ೞWindy City೮

Fiction Series
The Alex Evercrest Series
The River Front
The Girl on The Grill
Missing
Maggot
Racist
Votive Candles
Windy City
Country Road
Pool of Blood
Sins of the Daughter
Body Parts
The Skull Collector
The Vanishing
The Shadow Fighter
Moonshine
Grief's Trajectory
The Magic Touch
Northern Lights
Alex Evercrest Heroine
Alex Evercrest Collection Two
New Direction
A Family Affair
Disruption
The St. Lebuinnus Church Murder

A Brian O'Neil Novel
Hawaiian Phoenix
Moon Curser
Death Broker

The Problem Solver Series
Solutions
Drug Lords
Border Crosser
The Problem Solver Collection

The Taelo Series
Taelo: The Early Years
Taelo: The Golden Feather
Taelo: Journey of Discovery
Taelo: Dangerous Passage
Taelo: Condor Clan Slingers
Taelo: Circumvention
Taelo: The Journey of Sages
Taelo: Collection
Taelo: Future Leaders Journey
A Taelo Story:
White Swan and Quiet Pheasant
The Child's Name
Floating Cloud
Quiet Rabbit
Busy Bee
Little Otter & Talking Wren
Broken Spear
Burley Bear & Meadow Flower
Taelo Story Collection
Science Fiction

The Savitar Series:
Journey's End
Savitar
Confluence
Savitar Series Collection

Bram Nielson Series
The Fold
The Message
Fold Wormhole
Negative Fold
Ripples in Time
Bram Nielson Collection

Single Science Fiction Books:

Current Past and Future
The Event
The Door
Viajante 7

Ron Mueller

ೞWindy Cityೞ
By: Ron Mueller

Around the World Publishing LLC
Cincinnati, Ohio

This story is a work of fiction. Names, characters, places, and incidents either are products of the author's imagination or are used fictitiously. Any resemblance to actual events or locales or persons, living or dead, is entirely coincidental.

Windy City ©

ISBN 13: 978-1-68223-339-9

Distributed by Ingram
Alex Evercrest Model By: Pi03@ShutterStock
Cover Picture by: Checubus@ShutterStock
Cover Design By: Ron Mueller

Windy City

Ron Mueller

Dedicated to those who fight Organized crime.

Windy City

Ron Mueller

Windy City

1: Inside Man

The sun was threatening to come over the horizon. The misty fog hanging over the scene of the shooting gave it the feeling of evil.

This feeling of evil, lurking in wait, was not unique to only the Windy City but universal in both large and small cities. The history of this evil was rooted in the history of mankind.

It was the evil of projecting hate for those that were different.

Power was always a key differentiator.

With power came wealth and often wealth ushered in power.

Those in power looked down upon those below them. The discrimination that resulted was usually limited to making those below suffer by making them give more money to the rich.

The current evil that was in action was that of white against brown of any shade. It had been perpetrated by two men in blue for no other reason than they felt it was their right.

Jesse Franklin, deputy chief of police, ducked under the yellow security tape as he held out his badge for the young policewoman.

He had recently hired her and assigned her to this duty. He was sure this was her first murder crime scene.

The yellow taped area blocked off most of the corner of the intersection in a way that allowed traffic to be guided around the scene. An older model black Ford was at the center of the scene.

He walked over to the car and took in the young black man sitting in a pool of blood looking as if he were sleeping. He saw that a gun was still in the driver's right hand.

For a moment he watched the coroner examine the body of the driver. He noted that the blood pooled in the driver's seat had run down the drivers left leg. Jesse was sure that the driver had bled to death.

The driver was dressed as if he were going out for a run. He was not dressed as the typical drug dealer that Jesse normally saw.

The dispatcher had received a call about a drug dealer that had resisted arrest.

Jesse did not see a drug dealer.

He asked the coroner about the shooting.

The coroner told him that the man had been shot three times, once in the head and twice in the chest. He used his hand to show that the shots were from the driver's left side at what looked like a downward angle.

He went on and said that the wounds seemed to indicate the man had been shot while sitting in the driver's seat.

He leaned the driver up against the wheel and used a pointer and pushed it into what appeared to be a bullet hole.

The coroner said that they would likely find a bullet somewhere in the seat back.

What was clear to Jesse was that a young dead black man was about to be zipped into a body bag that the coroner's assistant had just wheeled up to the car.

He had seen too many similar cases. Usually, they were easier to accept as drug deals gone wrong. This scene and the coroner's showing him what appeared to be a bullet hole in the seat back pointed him to two rogue cops.

He looked around and saw the two policemen that had been involved. They were part of the group of cops that did a variety of shady errands that Jesse arranged for the Chicago Mafia. He wondered about this situation and what had really gone down.

He walked over and asked what had happened.

The story from the two police officers was that they had approached the car because of a broken taillight. They claimed the driver had opened the door of the vehicle and raised his gun to shoot at them. They shouted for him to drop his gun and when he didn't, they shot him, and he fell back into the driver's seat.

They went on to say that they had found a stash of drugs on the passenger side floor.

Jesse saw through the lie.

He was sure the two had set up the scene to make it look like they had shot a drug dealer. He decided not to challenge the two but to wait for the coroner's report before taking any action.

He knew that at a minimum he would assign these two to some district where they would not be involved in any more killing of young black men. The two would get the standard two weeks desk duty and then he would return them to street duty. At the moment that was all that he planned to do with the case.

He was glad that it was Friday, and he would not have to deal with the details of the incident until Monday.

He looked around the scene before leaving. The sun had broken over the horizon and had made the fluffy white clouds appear.

He loved the day night cycle and the atmosphere of living by the lake.

When he arrived back to his office, the flashing light on his phone seemed to emulate the flashing light of a police car.

He really disliked that light.

He pressed the button to hear the message. He let out an internal groan when he recognized it as a coded message from the office of the Chicago Mafia Boss, Gennaro Visentino.

Jesse thought of Gennaro as a true Mafia God Father figure.

He really did not need any complications on an already screwed up Friday morning.

He knew that he would have to contact him to see what Gennaro had in mind.

He turned off the voice mail. He opened his desk drawer and extracted one of his many burner phones from the back.

He then let his support know that he was going for a quick walk to unwind.

He was following a standard routine that he had practiced for many years. He never made calls to Gennaro from his office, and he never used the same phone more than once.

He walked toward the Lake and made his call.

Gennaro graciously thanked him for a quick response. It always impressed Jesse that Gennaro was always polite. Jesse also knew that Gennaro was just as deadly as he was polite.

What Gennaro had to say had his hair standing on end. It seemed that the office of the Illinois Lieutenant Governor was seeking to hire a Cincinnati police detective, Alex Evercrest, to investigate corruption in the Chicago police department.

This detective had earned national recognition for her ability to resolve every case she had been assigned to. She had experienced multiple attempts on her life and was recognized as a dead shot when she pulled her weapon.

Alarm bells went off in Jesse's head.

Jesse knew about one of her cases, just a couple of years ago, that had involved a coal barge that had lit up the Chicago skyline.

Single handedly she had taken out an attack gunship helicopter and destroyed a tug and coal barge.

The report was that she had been unarmed and fishing when the attack began

She had been unarmed when the DEA greeted her on her return to the fishing dock.

She claimed that she had been fishing and knew nothing about the burning barge.

The body count was said to be at least six, but no bodies had ever been recovered.

He brought his attention into focus as Gennaro asked him to call her and warn her not to accept the assignment. He wanted Jesse to make it clear in no uncertain terms that accepting the offer would mean certain retribution by the Chicago Mafia.

She was to understand that there would be not second chance to change her mind.

Jesse reacted negatively to making a call threatening the detectives life.

He did not want to be the one to make the call, but this was not a situation that he could say no to.

He preferred a controlled beating that allowed the person to feel the pain personally however he decide to obey Gennaro.

The had alarm bells kept going off in his head.

He would proceed with ultimate caution.

He had no other choice. He agreed to make the call.

The weekend was not going to be as relaxing as he had planned.

He had a nagging feeling about the situation.

He called an acquaintance on the Cincinnati police force and asked about the Black detective.

He learned that she always got the people involved in the case she was assigned to solve. He learned that she was very likeable and friendly and that her opponents seemed to underestimate her.

That evening he took a sleeping pill and went to sleep.

Even then he woke up several times.

The rest of the weekend seemed to drag. He went online and reviewed the stories about the black detective that he found in the national news snippets.

It gave him indigestion.

He took the pills for indigestion and heart burn, but they did him no good.

After reviewing her past accomplishments, he knew that she would not scare.

He was certain that his call would be a waste of his time.

He kept going over what he would say in when he warned her. He intuitively knew that it did not matter what or how he would say it and that she had a track record that said she did not scare.

Why make the call?

He remembered throwing a rock at a huge hornet's paper nest and watching the immediate surge of a black stream of small hornets heading straight for him.

They somehow were able to follow the trajectory of the rock.

He had the feeling that the phone call would be like throwing a stone at just as dangerous black detective.

He expected that this detective would follow the money trail. He felt that his lifestyle would put him under the magnifying glass. He was living in a luxury condominium and had a forty-five-foot yacht anchored in Burnham Harbor.

He had let his boss know about his "family inheritance" so that he could move into the luxury condo.

He later had purchased the yacht. At that time, he had let his associates at the station know that his parents had left him a small fortune.

He had been told that he was a lucky person to have parents that had been frugal and set him up for the good life.

There had been no inheritance, but it provided the cover he needed. The truth was he had to use his own money to pay for his parents funerals.

He had told his wife the same story about an inheritance. She had been surprised because she did not think his parents had much money to leave him, but she did not question it.

She loved the three thousand square foot condo he had leased and partying on the yacht.

She did not care much about going out of the harbor to go fishing so he usually did that with some of his work associates.

He had few personal friends and he kept it that way so that he did not have to explain his lifestyle.

All of his property, including a luxury condo in Miami, was registered under his wife's maiden name.

He felt confident in having covered his trail. He had made much of it public and the real money was offshore.

He had made sure that his personal bank account balanced with the income he made. He and his wife had modest investments in an IRA.

The money he "earned" with the mafia connection went to an offshore account in the Caymans and he seldom tapped into it. He was waiting until he left the department before touching it.

Jesse felt that he was secure in his personal position but what he had learned about Alex Evercrest's ability worried him.

He hoped that he would not have to throw too many of the cops that did his bidding under the bus.

It would be bad for his cash flow.

He came in on Monday and around nine he took one of his burner phones and went out for a walk.

He called the Cincinnati police station and asked for Alex Evercrest. He was on hold for a short time and then he heard a pleasant voice say, "May all be well with you, this is Alex how may I help you?"

He knew that in any other situation he would like her. She had perfect diction and it was clear she was very friendly.

The hornets coming out of their nest flashed in his mind. They were small and their buzz was almost un hearable.

He tried to hide his real voice by deepening his tone, he told her that accepting a position to root out corruption in the Chicago Police Force would endanger her life and the lives of her loved ones.

He was surprised at her chuckle and her response of thanking him for helping her make up her mind. She then went on to say that the two of them would soon meet and he should be ready to spend a great portion of his future life behind bars.

He then heard a click.

She had ended the call!

Her response put him in as state of panic.

She had reacted in a much more aggressive way than he had expected.

And she seemed so sure she would know who he was.

He took out a second burner phone and called Gennaro, let him know that his call had landed on deaf ears and that the Cincinnati detective had indicated she planned to accept coming to Chicago to root out the spoiled eggs that were on the police force.

He looked out toward the lake as the silence reverberated through his head.

He felt some sense of relief when he heard Gennaro say that he would take care of the Cincinnati detective and that he should relax because she would never make it to Chicago.

He liked the way Gennaro was choosing to deal with the situation.

He envisioned a fly being splattered by a fly swatter.

He returned to the office. His support handed him the coroner's initial report. He carefully read through it and knew that the two cops had killed an innocent man.

He put in a call to check on the victim's previous arrest records. There were none. He knew of no drug dealers with no arrest records.

A call from the Internal Affairs letting him know that they were looking into the shooting made it clear that he needed to get the two officers off the force. He knew Internal Affairs would find out the same information that he had.

He called in the two cops. He asked them again to tell him what had happened. It was clear that the two had spent the morning embellishing their story.

They handed him a written report. They had the black driver getting out of the car and then reaching for his gun. They had immediately called out, "police, you are under arrest and then as his gun came out, one of them had shot him twice in the chest and the other shot him once in the head.

As he listened, he picked up the coroner's report that clearly indicated the shots had been at an angle that indicated the shooters were standing and shooting down at the victim.

The two officers had made up their stories. They were lying to him. It seemed to him that the two probably killed an innocent person and tried to make it look like a drug bust.

He looked at them and told them to read the coroner's report and that they had an appointment with Internal Affairs.

He advised them to improve their story telling and that at least the lies should match the facts that were in the Coroner's report.

He then suggested they resign, walk out of the office, and go find jobs elsewhere.

He asked them for their guns and assigned them to two weeks of desk duty. He was washing his hands of their case.

He was throwing them under the bus.

The two said that they were resigning and would find jobs elsewhere.

He was relieved. He felt he had more important things to worry about.

He had no idea that the more important worry was coming at him faster than he anticipated.

He was totally blind to the fact that Alex Evercrest's mother was the one that had created the tsunami of catastrophes that was about to overtake his life.

He should have paid closer attention to the name of the lawyer that had asked for the police reports on the case cops who were being prosecuted for shooting a black driver of a car stopped for speeding. If he had paid closer attention, he would have linked Alex Evercrest with her mother, Rose Ann Evercrest, the lawyer who had repeatedly asked for information that he had blocked.

2 Connections

Rose Anne took pride in winning her cases for her clients. Her practice grew as her win record became known She represented many affluent white clients but made it a policy that she would represent an equal number of black or people of color.

Her practice of doing ten percent pro-bono work turned out to be the best public advertisement that she had for her business. She made a point that her pro-bon work also crossed the color barrier and made sure that at least seventy percent went for those most discriminated against.

She had several young lawyers that she had hired because she felt they were among the best she could find. She had always made the claim that the best people represented the least expense for a business because their successes generated more income.

Her monetary compensation for the best put her employees among the highest paid in the Chicago legal system. It also made them among the most loyal employees.

Rose-Anne knew many of the details of Alex's successful cases. She had been horrified by the flaming spectacle that Alex had lived through out on the lake when Alex had single handed destroyed a helicopter gunship, burned a barge and the tug pushing it and had killed at least five.

She had been aboard the yacht that carried the entire Cincinnati detective unit out to go fishing. Then as they were fishing, she watched in amazement as Alex dodged bullets to get everyone to safety. Alex then used her skill to disable the speed boat of the attacker. When they got to the peer, she saw the blood dripping from Alex's gun hand as she ran up the dock to try and stop the attacker.

She always knew her daughter was very good at what she chose to do. It was then that she realized that her daughter was phenomenal, and she was an attack dog when threatened.

She was aware of and thought that Alex had even taken out the leader of the Gulf Cartel. That was a case where Trey had almost been killed and Alex was out for payback. She however knew that after that case, a new cartel boss made his appearance.

Rose Anne had come to realize that her daughter was both brilliant in mind, deadly in fighting crime and she was one of the best across the entire country.

When she learned that a local Cincinnati lawyer had been able to get her to help him on two cases, Rose Ann decided that she would see if she could arrange for Alex to deal with the broken Chicago Police force.

She was frustrated with dealing with the case of three policemen accused of killing an innocent driver that had been stopped for speeding.

The shooting had been captured on video from an overpass by a person who happened to be walking across at the time of the arrest. The video seemed to indicate that it would be an open and shut case.

After taking on the case, she had asked for the police reports and for any other evidence that had been gathered.

She was stonewalled.

She came away empty handed.

She had submitted her request to the top Chicago Police leaders with no result.

She decided that something had to be done to clean up the system. The police department seemed to have become a law onto itself.

They did whatever they wanted.

She reached out to her college roommate friend, Jane Stradford, who had been elected as the Illinois Lieutenant Governor.

The two agreed that a lucrative offer for Alex's services to come for a special assignment to root out corrupt police was a great idea.

Jane commented that it would stretch her budget but if she could make a dent in eliminating the corruption, she felt it would be worth it.

She said that she would make the best offer that she could and hoped that it would be attractive to both Alex and her bosses.

Jane commented that she knew how tight her budget was and figured that the police budget in Cincinnati would be just as tight and they would welcome a generous financial arrangement.

She put together the offer and sent it out so it would be in Alex's boss's hands on Monday morning.

On Monday both of them were surprised that Alex's initial inclination was to turn down the offer but that she would spend the day to think about it and consider it.

Rose-Anne let Russel know about her request to have Alex come to Chicago to root out bad cops and about Alex's hesitation.

He had responded that he thought as a mother she should not be asking her daughter to take on the Chicago mafia.

It was as dangerous as facing a helicopter gunship with a fishing pole.

Rose Anne's response was that she had not asked her to take on the Mafia but to look for bad cops.

Russel replied with a question, "Who do you think bad cops work for? Their Mafia bosses will not take it lightly and they control their environment with violence."

This stopped the reply she had been thinking of giving him because of his gunship remark.

She had overlooked that obvious Mafia connection.

She was disturbed as she walked away after the discussion.

Not long after, her Alex chimes came from her phone.

When Alex asked if she had been the catalyst that had triggered the request for her services from the Illinois Lieutenant Governor's office, she replied that she indeed had been but that she was now thinking it was not such a good idea.

She told Alex to turn down the request.

She was not expecting to hear Alex laugh and reply that she intended to accept on the condition that she and her detective partner were hired by the Lieutenant Governor and would be employees of the state of Illinois for as long as the assignment lasted. She was encouraging her boss to accept the lucrative compensation offer for such an arrangement.

Rose-Anne again said that she was sorry about having the request made and tried to dissuade Alex, but she knew that she had no chance of do so.

She again heard Alex laugh and was told that the price of having thought of such an arrangement was that she planned to work from home.

Rose Anne felt great about that the idea but kept quiet.

She listened as Alex went on and let her know that Trey's family would be coming up on weekends to stay at the house. They would be using one to the bedrooms.

Alex also mentioned that her dad should consider going fishing on most weekends.

Rose Anne liked everything she heard.

She was now a concerned mother versus the successful prosecutor that had recruited her daughter into a dangerous role. She said that she would do all she could to make sure Alex would get the support she needed.

Rose-Anne called Jane and shared the fact that Alex would only accept the request if she and her current partner were hired by the Lieutenant Governor's office for a one-year period of pay at their current salary and that the original monetary offer was to be separately given to the Cincinnati Detective Unit.

Rose-Ann listened as Jane replied that for her it was a no brainer. She would love to have someone like Alex working for her department for a year. However, she would need to check her budget to see how she would work it out.

Work sucked Rose-Anne back in and she was consumed in trying to get the information she needed to proceed with the case against the three policemen.

She requested a delay of the trial until the documents she needed were made available. The judge agreed to a two-month delay.

It was the breather she was looking for.

She let her staff know about the delay and asked them to handle the smaller cases that were underway.

She planned to use the week to prepare for Alex and Trey's arrival.

She turned her attention to getting the house ready.

Rose-Anne was warming up to the idea of having Alex working from home and wondered how long such an arrangement would last.

She hoped that it would indeed be a year.

She watched as Russel tuned and polished Alex's twelve-cylinder Jaguar.

They both knew that it was a treasure that Alex loved.

She then noted that he also inspected and prepared all the fishing equipment. Fishing had been an activity that he and Alex had shared and enjoyed since she was a little girl.

She listened as he called to have their boat tuned up and put back in the water.

The owner of the boat docks at the harbor was almost as excited as Russel about having Alex back to go fishing and even offered his personal yacht and jokingly commented that he only asked that this time it be returned without bullet holes in it.

This was in reference to the last time he had rented the boat to Russel when the entire Cincinnati detective team had gone fishing and a shooter had put at least a dozen holes into the boat.

Rose Ann continued to worry but she knew that Alex would call her own shots and make her own deal.

She had no idea of the risk and the carnage that Alex was about to experience.

And she had no idea about the kind of loyal and powerful supporters Alex was surrounded by.

She would have been pleased to know that Alex's boss Bruce, Chief of Detectives, and his wife Mary-Ann thought of Alex as the daughter they never had and they were constantly discussing how to keep her safe.

3 *The Chief*

*T*he Cincinnati Detective unit had been lily white until he was recruited to take the role as Chief. He had been hired to help integrate the Cincinnati detective unit.

He recognized that he was the first Black Chief of detectives and the first cog in the integration engine.

He was informed that he should recruit some Black detectives.

His first action was to have a personal one-on-one with each of the current detectives. He made a point of asking them what the barriers were for them to do their best and for him to provide the kind of support he could give them.

He did not get much that was of help.

When he first started, the team that stood out to him was the team made up of Bill and Travis.

He knew that Bill had put in a bid to become Chief. In his one-on-one discussion with Bill, he had asked Bill about his feelings about having been rejected for the role of Chief after so many good years of service and now having to work for a Black Chief.

He listened as Bill said that he did not like it and that he was waiting to see if he would be a supporter of his new Boss. He qualified that by saying that he was not going to do anything negative, but he needed to see how things worked out before becoming a full supporter.

Bruce thanked Bill for expressing himself and asked Bill for his support. Bruce was later pleased that Bill became one of his staunchest supporters.

His partner Travis was harder to read. He was the perfect partner for Bill because he was not interested in taking the lead. Travis's mode of interaction with his co-workers was to harass them verbally and jokingly.

Bruce searched for another black detective candidate to lead a detective team. None of the few Black Police officers in the Police Department put in for the role.

He was impressed with the resume of a young black female deputy, Alex Evercrest, that a sheriff from a small town in northern Illinois recommended. Her boss was the one that sent in the response to his add with a recommendation letter that blew him away.

He wished that he would have had such a boss to work for.

He was even more impressed when he had an interview with the person that had been recommended.

He had asked her for a face-to-face interview in Cincinnati.

When she walked in, he saw her petite figure and wondered if he would hire someone of such small stature.

She threw a giant shadow as she went through the interview.

After the interview, he offered her the highest salary that he was allowed.

The inability to get someone from within the Cincinnati Police Force to become her partner was the next surprise.

Bill informed him that the word was out that anyone putting in to be a partner with the new Black female detective would be "blackballed."

He assured the Chief there would be no volunteers.

He said he would take the role if there was no other choice.

Bruce thanked him but let him know that he was going to recruit someone from outside of the department.

He was pleased to hire Trey McGregor from the Minneapolis police.

He was impressed with the fact that Trey's resume included his history as a Marine. Trey had received a purple heart and the medal of valor for his action is saving a platoon that was trapped by enemy fire.

He was not surprised that Trey became Alex's best friend and that she soon became, "Aunt" to his son, Nolan.

He was sitting in the office contemplating the assignments that the three detective teams under his supervision. There were more investigations than there were people to carry them out. He had asked for another team, but the budget crunch had caused that request to be turned down.

He was trying to make up his mind about the assignments when his support handed him a message coming from the Illinois Lieutenant Governor.

He read the request and was astonished at the financial offer that was being proposed to have Alex work for her.

The first thing he did was to ask his support how she had received the offer. She said that it had been an e-mail from the office of the Illinois Lieutenant Governor.

He looked out to the bull pen to see if there were any signs of Trevor, his known prankster, to see if he was looking like he was waiting for his reaction.

He wanted to check to make sure he was not being set up.

He didn't see anything that seemed unusual, but he called Trevor into his office.

Trevor assured him he had nothing to do with any request from the Lieutenant Governor of Illinois. He volunteered that he thought he knew the detective that was being asked for.

Bruce decided to call the Lieutenant Governor's office and make sure the offer was legitimate.

But he was going to give himself time and take a break first.

He thanked Trevor and suggested it was time for a cup of coffee and led the way to the coffee pot.

Bill and Trevor always brought in donuts. Today he decided that a bear claw and a cup of coffee were in order before he made the call to the Illinois Lieutenant Governor's office.

He looked over the request again. The offer included an up-front sum of money that would allow him to fund at least one additional detective team. It specifically named Alex Evercrest as the detective that the Lieutenant Governor wanted. The assignment was to investigate and expose the crooked cops on the Chicago Police Force.

His initial reaction was that he should turn down the request for two reasons.

He had a full workload for his department and for Alex and Trey, who had proved to be his best team.

The second reason was that the Chicago assignment was a huge risk.

He also noted that the request did not ask for Trey. He knew that Alex would not accept an situation that did not include him.

Alex's successes had elevated his political standing.

She always identified him as the reason she succeeded.

She had made his dream of becoming Cincinnati Mayor something that now seemed like it might be possible.

Closer to his current situation was his attempt at making his position, The Chief of Detectives a position equal to the Chief of Police department.

Mary-Anne often reminded him that hiring Alex was the best thing he had done as Chief.

The second best was to hire Trey who was not only a decorated war hero but the most loyal partner that Alex could have.

She told him to have the confidence that Alex would make the right choice.

He should give her the choice.

The request he held in his hands would bolster his influence in the police department and it would provide badly needed funding.

Russel knew he was being taunted by the devil.

He looked out and saw that Alex was now at her desk. He went to the door and asked her to come in for a discussion.

He made the point of closing the windows and the door.

He held out the request and asked her to read it.

He watched for her reaction. There was a moment of silence as she scanned the request document.

He realized that she was a speed reader and that she grasped all the details in record time.

He was surprised when she said that her mother had just reached out and praised her. She shared that the Illinois Lieutenant Governor was her mother's college roommate. She went on to say that the praise was that her mother always said that "she only went after the best."

He was not surprised when she said that the offer was certainly a great offer, but the risks were monumental.

Russel looked at her and asked if her mother always asked the best to go in to face angry lions.

He listened as Alex made the point that the offered sum for her services was impressive and would make a significant positive impact on his budget.

She looked at him and asked if he were asking her to accept the assignment.

He said that he was asking her to consider it, but he thought it was extremely dangerous and that he was inclined to reject it.

He listened as she said that she was enticed by the offer but not sure she would take it on and if she did, she would want to put in additional conditions.

She looked at him and said that she was going to ask for the opinions of her supporters and ask them for ways that might make the assignment successful.

He agreed to Alex's request for four copies of the request by the Illinois Lieutenant Governor. He watched her go back to her desk where she talked to Johnnie and seemed to give him an assignment.

Bruce called in his support and asked her to make copies of the request.

He then called the Chief of Police to make him aware of the offer put forward by the Illinois Lieutenant Governor.

He wanted to make sure that no issues would arise if Alex did accept.

He was assured that he would get support all the way to the Cincinnati Mayor. The request for Alex was a feather in the Police Department's and Cincinnati's cap.

Bruce was sure a success in Chicago would open a new door to how Alex and the Cincinnati Detective unit would be viewed and utilized.

There was no doubt in his mind that it would be a feather in his cap as well.

Not long after, he was surprised when Johnnie invited him to be part of a lunch that Alex had asked him to schedule.

It pleased him to be included, and he offered to drive to the restaurant.

He had at least an hour before the lunch meeting.

He picked up the phone and dialed the office of the Illinois Lieutenant Governor.

He informed her that he appreciated the generous offer and that he was on the side of declining, but that Alex had called together the people she considered her support team to advise her over a lunch meeting. He let her know that he would call later in the afternoon.

Little did Russel know that the road ahead would get brighter for he and his organization nor had he any idea of how deadly the world around Alex would become.

4 The Price of Fame

*T*he lull at work had been a welcome respite. Alex had enjoyed the day at Trey's where she got to play with Nolan, and his two close friends Linda and Lorie.

Their mothers were now good friends and spent many weekends together.

She took every opportunity to be the person that the kids loved to play with. They called her "Aunt Alex" and for that they got a treat every time.

She welcomed and accepted every invitation Trey made He boasted that she was the best babysitter he had, and she was free.

She laughed at that and said that the only reason she kept coming over was because of the great food Lindsey prepared and that she accepted his brats and beer because she didn't want him to feel bad.

She enjoyed the back-and-forth banter that she and Trey constantly threw at each other.

They had solid work relationship and a very close personal one as well. And they were now AA partners as well.

She and Matt had spent Sunday, from brunch to late lunch, at Trey's. They were now back at her apartment sitting on the couch. She was leaning against him and enjoying a glass of her favorite, alcohol free, Spumanti.

Matt joked with her about the fact that he had to give up some of the best wine in the world because of her allergy to Alcohol. What he referred to as an allergy was the fact that Alex was a member of AA and planned to be a successful one for life.

She blamed her excessive partying during her first couple of years in college for making her feel like an alcoholic. She had joined AA and decided to become alcohol free. She knew it was the right move.

She had fallen in love with Matt the first time she had looked into his mesmerizing green eyes.

She knew that she had met her mate in an atypical situation. The meeting had been in the back of an ambulance rushing to the hospital with the person she had shot.

When they arrived at the hospital, he had invited her for a cup of coffee in the hospital cafeteria. She accepted and during that first coffee, she almost lost him when the person they had brought in attacked them.

The attack had ended in the attacker laying at her feet with a hole between her eyes.

She was grazed by the one shot the attacker managed to get off.

Matt made her sit down while he bandaged her wound.

She knew that their meeting was unconventional and that some hand from above must have intervened on her behalf.

She was even more amazed when Matt had surprised her by moving to Cincinnati so that he could continue to date her.

He had not only dated her, but he had also been on duty when his EMT team had transported her to the emergency room when the angry mother and father of the mobster she had killed, shot her.

She later learned that the bullet just missed a critical artery otherwise she would have died.

Another hand from above.

The rapid transport to the hospital was credited with having saved her. Matt was the first person she saw when she came to in her hospital bed.

That moment was now a distant memory among many better moments she had shared with Matt.

She snuggled against him and pulled his head toward her so she could give him a kiss. She quietly thanked him for being willing to spend quiet evenings relaxing and just talking and chatting.

She wished that he could spend the night, but she knew that he was on duty that evening.

The next morning the coffee infused her with energy. She hoped the rest of the day would make her feel as good.

She checked her bike to make sure it was ready to go. She pushed it down the hall to the elevator.

The ride down was smooth, but she could hear the faint clicks of the guide wheels going over what she thought of as weld bumps. When she closed her eyes, she thought of a train going click-clack down the track.

When the doors slid open, she greeted, Johnnie who was standing and waiting with his bike.

Since she had been attacked on one of her rides to work, Johnnie had become the lead person on their ride to the station.

They had three different routes that they chose to ride and used the flip of a coin each morning to select which route they would ride.

Alex teased Johnnie about being old and slow, but she simply admired his attitude and the fact that he was a very good rider. He said that he had been point when he was in Vietnam when his unit went out on patrol.

Alex saw him as a magician at using the various official data bases and the internet to ferret out information that always seemed to guide her to solve her cases.

She was glad that he had stopped her and asked her to listen to what he knew about the young lady that had been thrown off the overpass in front of a semi.

She had listened to him, and she had hired him when he demonstrated his skills.

This morning, they were riding the most direct route that took them by Cincinnati's Main library.

This was the route that she had been riding when a bright blue pickup with a person shooting his AR-15 seemed to fill the air with bullets. She was able to take refuge behind an old Cadillac that ended up looking like a metal version of Swiss cheese. When the pickup drove past, she stood up and shot and killed both the shooter and the driver as the truck was about to turn the corner.

The attackers were dead, but the organizer of the attack continued the assault on her until she tracked him down and in a gun battle, he too was killed.

She was still seeing a psychologist to deal with the fact that the attack had been unprovoked and was due to the color of her skin.

It was hatred and prejudice at its extreme.

On this morning, she and Johnnie arrived at the station later than usual. She had spent too much time enjoying her morning shower and her cup of coffee.

Instead of being the first in the office, she and Johnnie were the last ones to enter the detective bull pen. They both stopped for their morning cup of coffee and had split the last blue berry muffin.

She was expecting Travis to make some a snide remark about her late arrival.

The absence of a tease immediately heightened her senses.

She sensed something was up.

She looked at Trey and his casual poker face sealed the fact.

She turned to where Johnnie was sitting and asked him if he sensed the tension in the air.

Johnnie smiled and said that if they were in battle, he would be telling her to dig a deep fox hole and keep her head down.

She was turning back to her desk when the Chief appeared in the door to his office and waved to her over.

Alex looked back around at the four and then walked to the Chief's office. He closed the door and then closed the blinds. This Alex knew was his way of telling her that he had an unusual situation that concerned her and that he was not sure how she would react.

He held up an official looking letter and pointed to the header. It was a letter from the Office of the Illinois Lieutenant Governor.

He turned and handed her a copy of the letter and asked her to read it and let him know what she thought.

Alex flipped to the last page. She wanted to know who had signed it. She recognized the name and knew that her mother was the catalyst for the request.

She looked back at the Chief and asked when he had received the letter. He replied that he been handed the letter just this morning when he arrived at the office.

Alex sat down and went slowly through the letter.

She was surprised that the Lieutenant Governor was offering an amount four times her salary to compensate for her absence from the department.

She knew that the Chief had been struggling with the workload, and he had been denied the funds to hire more detectives.

She figured the offer would allow him to hire at least one more team.

She looked up at him and asked what his reply had been.

The Chief looked at her and said that only the two of them knew of the offer details and that he had made sure it was not a prank being pulled by Trevor.

She thanked him for sharing it with her before deciding. He told her that he would respond to the offer based on her response.

Alex looked at the Chief and said that she would need to think about it and that she wanted Trey's, Johnnie's, Bill's, and Travis's opinions about taking on a case of rooting out corruption in the Chicago Police Department and identifying the bad cops.

Bruce responded that he would wait until she came back to him with her position before making a reply. He let her know that she would have the final say.

Alex held up the letter and asked for four additional copies The Chief said that his support would make the copies for her

Alex walked out of the office and went back to her desk. It was clear to her that Trey and the rest were expecting an explanation about what had gone on in the office.

She was about to explain when the Chief's assistant brought the copies of the request.

She took a moment to hand out the request from the Illinois Lieutenant Governor and said that she wanted their opinion but that she wanted to wait until they had all enjoyed lunch at one of Johnnie's favorite restaurants.

Travis gave a chuckle and commented that Johnnie always picked the most expensive restaurants as one of his favorites.

She listened as Johnnie denied that and that this time, he was picking a restaurant with a good river view.

She asked him to see if the Chief wanted to go with them and then make reservations for a noon lunch.

Alex nodded to Trey and asked him to go with her for a cup of coffee.

Trevor looked at her and commented that the assignment must be a real doozy if she was springing for lunch.

She replied that it was that and more.

She placed a call to Matt and asked if he could take a break and join Trey and her for coffee at Peetz.

She and Trey walked to the small coffee shop and took a table in the corner. Matt arrived a few moments later.

The three were sitting at the table waiting for their orders when Alex handed Matt the request from the Illinois Lieutenant Governor.

Matt scanned it and asked whether it was a real offer and even if it was, she would be crazy to accept it.

Trey had a slightly different reaction.

He said the offer was not enough, that it was too dangerous and that he would not let her do it alone.

He said that he knew his partner well enough and suspected she would accept.

He said that if she took the case, he demanded to be her backup. He reminded her that they were a team.

Alex looked at Trey and reminded him that he had to think about his family.

Trey replied that Lindsey would back him one hundred and fifty percent and Nolan would insist that he protect his aunt.

He went on and said that there was no way he would not go with her. He would make a public scene if it were necessary.

Matt said that he would support her no matter what the decision but that he supported Trey's position two hundred percent.

Alex looked at the two and smiled and told them that she loved them both.

She let Trey know that if she accepted the assignment, she would insist that he be part of the package.

She let them know that she was not yet sure she would take on such an overwhelming challenge.

She had mixed emotions about taking the assignment and was going to decide after she had heard what they all had to say after lunch.

She also made the point that she would insist that Johnnie, Bill, and Trevor would support her. They would stay in Cincinnati but be available.

They all agreed that Johnnie should be the information sleuth and that Bill and Trevor might know some of the police force members and be able to provide some insight to the internal situation with the Chicago Police Department.

Alex reminded them that they would meet for lunch at noon but that they would all have to check with Johnnie to learn what restaurants he had selected.

She said that she was going for a walk to the waterfront and call her mother.

She took her time and thought about how to confront her mother.

On the one hand she knew that her mother had praised her but that her mother was putting her into one of the most dangerous situations that she could imagine.

Her mother at first tried to deflect the question of how the Illinois Lieutenant Governor had come up with the idea of making an offer for her services.

Alex pressed the point and reminded her mother that the Lieutenant Governor had been her roommate in college and that she had been at the house for the high school graduation party a few years ago.

Alex then listened as her mother shared the frustration of bad cops framing her clients and then doing the same thing to some other poor individual.

She pointed out that Alex had worked on a case outside of the normal detective's office authority, and that she thought Alex could make a significant dent in the behavior of the Chicago Police Department.

Alex recalled that her mother always made the point that she only recruited the best. She knew that she was receiving the highest praise her mother could bestow.

She wondered if her mother knew that taking on the Chicago Police Department was like being a small Nordic Clan that was taking on the Roman Army.

It was like David facing Goliath.

She was currently thinking that the assignment was close to committing suicide.

She knew that if she accepted the offer, she would need a miracle to make it through alive.

She thought for a minute and knew that Johnnie would need to do what no one had done so far in dealing with the police corruption in Chicago had been able to do. He would need to identify the bad guys in blue and be able to provide her with the information that she could use to act at the speed of light.

5: Super Sleuth

J ohnnie knew that Alex had given him a second chance at life.

She was the most dynamic and caring person that he had ever met.

Alex was the person that had turned his downward trajectory to an upward one.

He knew that Alex was young enough to be the granddaughter he never had.

For him, her petite figure cast a giant blazing shadow.

As far as he was concerned she was ten feet tall.

He had witnessed a young woman being thrown from an overpass.

The wrong person was arrested.

He tried to come forward as a witness only to be ignored.

He was aware of the young policewoman that rode her bike past the Cincinnati Main Library each morning.

He stopped her to see if she would listen.

She had looked past his humble cloths and wrinkled skin and had had listened and believed him.

She had not only believed him, but she had also saved him when the thug that had thrown the young woman off the overpass had tracked him down.

She shot and killed him when he refused to put down his gun. Johnnie remembered that as the thug died he seemed to bow down to her before he collapsed on the floor.

The thug's mother in her attempt to avenge her son had destroyed Alex's apartment with a rocket launched grenade. He had been relieved to learn that Alex had been down in the gym running.

He saw a hand from above.

He realized that during his time utilizing the computers in the library and hacking into various systems he had developed an uncanny ability to break through most firewalls that protected large data basis.

He had not sought to be a hacker; he just needed to get around without having to give all the information the systems were always seeking to extract from him.

Alex had hired him as data base analyst when he demonstrated his hacking skills.

He had been able to provide Alex with the critical information that case after case led to her success.

When her partner was beaten to the point he was in a coma. Johnnie had stepped up and insisted that he back her up in her pursuit of the bad guys.

The two of them had faced a helicopter gunship and together they caused it to crash and explode. The incident had surfaced Alex's uncanny ability to overcome the most challenging of situations and had also exposed bravery that he had not seen since Vietnam.

On that case he had met Mary and late in life he now had a budding romance.

He thought about the movie where the old man slowly grew younger.

In his later years, Alex had given him the things that he had missed during his youth.

He felt as young and vigorous as when he had been in his twenties.

He brought his thoughts to the present.

He read slowly through the official looking document that Alex had given him. As he comprehended that significant positive impact the money being offered for her services, would have on the Cincinnati Detective Unit, he knew that she would accept the assignment.

He knew she would accept what he thought of as a suicide case.

His mind began to immediately think through how he would research and identify the bad cops.

What worried him most was that he knew that the Mafia ran the city and that the worst of the bad cops worked for them.

That meant that she would also raise the anger of the local Mafia boss.

He began immediately to think through the information that he knew she would need to be successful.

He swore to himself that he would supply the information, and he knew that she would leverage it to its fullest.

He turned his attention back to getting the lunch meeting that Alex had requested him to set up.

He verified that the Chief wanted to attend and then decided on where the lunch would be.

He enjoyed being able to select from a wide variety of good restaurants that graced downtown Cincinnati.

He selected one of the restaurants with a view of the river and the Kentucky waterfront.

The river view always provided some sort of interesting visual action.

The morning then seemed to creep by. He left his desk and began to do research on the situation in the Chicago police department.

What he discovered alarmed him.

The corruption seemed to be tolerated as if it was normal.

It was a tsunami meets a hurricane on the shore of Lake Michigan, and everyone seemed to accept it as normal.

He was sure that people high on the food chain had to be corrupt.

Alex returned just before it was time to head to the river front for lunch.

He, Alex, Trey, Bill, Trevor, accepted a ride with the Chief. It was a little tight, but it was a short ride.

When they entered the restaurant, they were taken to their table. He was pleased that his request for a river view was exactly as he had envisioned it.

Once the orders were in, he listened closely as Alex asked for each of their opinions and suggestions.

Johnnie knew why he was at the table.

He would be asked to deliver miracles.

He had wondered about Bill and Travis, but it became clear to him that they knew a significant number of the Chicago Police Department personnel.

He now looked at them as providing him with special leads to guide his information search.

He asked some clarifying questions as he sought a way to set up his search parameters.

When Alex turned to him and asked for his opinion, he replied that he thought she was crazy to take it on but that he would give her the information on both bad cops and who the mafia members were.

He would be focused on getting her the intel that she would need to be one step ahead of the bad guys and to stay alive.

He looked at the Chief and asked if he would support him in using his time in that manner.

The Chief nodded and replied that he would not only support him but would make sure that he had access to any system he needed.

After dessert he suggested that Alex and he spend some time to aim his online search.

She said that she would get with him when she got back to the office.

He watched as Alex left the restaurant with Matt and said she was walking back to the station.

He had not paid attention to when Matt had come in, but he knew that her walk back with him was the pivotal discussion that would determine if she took the case.

The rest of them rode back with the Chief.

When the Chief looked at him and asked if he thought Alex would take on the assignment, Johnnie replied that the conversation she was having with Matt would probably determine the answer.

It seemed to be about an hour later when he watched Alex come into the work area and walk straight into the Chief's office.

He watched as Trey went into the huddle room. He waited a few moments and then went in.

He shared his thinking of how to identify bad cops and asked Trey if he had any other ideas.

Trey said that he had a few previous acquaintances that were on the Chicago police force, and he would reach out to them.

He said that following the money trail would most likely be the way to find bad cops, but he was sure that the worst ones would have figured out ways to hide their money trail.

Johnnie agreed.

He replied that he had learned that most people trying to hide money would use their younger relatives as places to park money.

Distant older relatives seemed to also be in favor.

A few had would have good friends that would provide hiding places.

In all cases the individuals providing a way to hide money thought they were helping by keeping the government from over taxing their more fortunate relative or friend.

Once back at his desk, Johnnie put together an action plan. He had observed the way that Alex had entered and walked directly to the Chief's office and closed the door.

He knew then that Alex would take on the assignment and that she worked at a very fast pace. He would have to put in some marathon search time so that he could give her as much ammo as possible.

Alex was in the Chief's office longer than he expected.

He had already done an initial search and was sure he had found the top bad cop.

He wondered how such an obvious situation could have been overlooked.

He wondered where that person was getting his support.

When Chief came to the door and waved for Trey to come into his office, Johnnie knew that Alex had accepted the assignment.

He anxiously waited to hear about what the final arrangements that Alex would undoubtedly negotiate.

He focused his efforts on finding out the name of the Chicago mafia boss. He again was surprised how quickly he found the information he was after.

In both cases, Johnnie found out that independent news reporters had done a thorough job at uncovering detailed facts about the individuals he was interested in.

He figured these reporters must have wondered why they were being ignored. He mentally thanked them for giving him a quick start on his information search.

He felt that he had his first small miracle.

Trey and Alex walked out of the Chief's office and Johnnie was surprised to have the Chief wave Bill, Trevor, and he into the office.

They walked in and the Chief closed the door.

The Chief explained that the Illinois Lieutenant Governor was going to swear in Alex and Trey as officers of the State of Illinois. The three of them were to be witnesses to the swearing in procedure.

He was surprised by the speed at which all of it was happening, but he knew it was most likely being driven by Alex.

After the swearing in ceremony, he learned that she and Trey would be going to Chicago on Friday. Once there they would meet with the Chief of Police and set up an office at the main police station and begin in earnest on Monday.

Johnnie was pleased that Alex had negotiated for the state of Illinois to pay for his search efforts.

He gave a small laugh and told the Chief that they already owned him for three hours of work.

He asked the Chief what he thought about the assignment and was not surprised to hear the Chief declare that it was suicide but that his suicide Angel had survived the other assignments that he had thought extremely dangerous.

Johnnie asked the Chief if he had any contacts at the Chicago police department.

He walked out of the Chief's office and noted that the Chief asked Bill and Travis to stay for a moment.

Johnnie wondered what their role would be.

He had already established their value, but he was sure that Alex had likely monetized their support as well and he wondered how the Chief planned to make it all work.

He had it right.

He had no idea just how critical his information would be.

He also wondered how Trey planned to be the good father and husband and be the backup that Alex would need.

He would soon learn how close Alex was with Trey's family.

He would soon learn that he indeed had supplied both Alex and Trey with the information that would deliver the first miracle.

6 Partner

*T*he room stood still as Trey read the offer put forward by the Illinois Lieutenant Governor. He was in shock as he comprehended the magnitude of the assignment, and the danger involved.

His battles in Afghanistan seemed like kids game as compared to what she was facing in Chicago.

It was a very generous proposal to obtain the her services

His name was not mentioned.

He knew that he would not let her go on her own even if he had to resign and go with her on his own. He was her partner and friend.

He corrected himself: she was more than a friend.

His son, Nolan, called her "Aunt Alex" and adored her.

His wife, Lindsey, credited Alex with saving both his emotional life and later his physical life.

She and Nolan had also been saved by Alex.

He had been the one that had given her the moniker, "Cincinnati's Black Annie Oakley" that Matt had used in Wiggins.

When she fired her weapon, she hit what she intended to.

She was fast, accurate and if she were cutting notches in the handle of here weapon there would be no handle.

He knew she was one step above him in skill, determination, and bravery.

He knew her to be generous to all people but to be brutal with those that chose to attack her or anyone in her sphere.

He knew that Alex would accept the case.

She thrived on what initially appeared as an impossible case and then on finding the solution.

She also did it in record time.

He figured that her speed always caught the perpetrator off balance. It was a balance that often had the perps falling off the cliff of their own making.

The solution path was often riddled with the bodies of the bad guys that had underrated her and tried to kill her.

He was sitting at the lunch that Alex had set up. He looked out over the river and knew that he could not let her take on the case by herself.

He was her work partner and together they had survived some difficult cases. He still had some lingering effects from the drug case where he received a brutal beating that nearly killed him.

She somehow was able to help him escape and then she had killed all but one of their captors.

He still thought of it as a miracle delivered by a Black Angel.

That Angel was his partner.

He was her partner and would stand with her in all situations.

He watched her leave the restaurant with Matt and figured that the two of them would discuss the impact of the case on their relationship.

And he knew that relationship was a bond of two souls meant to be with each other.

Not long after getting back to the office, he watched Alex go into the Chief's office. She had not looked at anyone in the bullpen, so he knew she had reached a decision.

It was time to get Lindsey on board and get her reaction to his thinking. He went into a huddle room and called.

He read her the official request from the Illinois Lieutenant Governor.

When he stopped reading, he was relieved to hear Lindsey say that he had to go with Alex.

She made the point that Alex had saved his life and had taken on a drug cartel to punish them for having almost killed him.

She pointed out that Alex had become family.

She then pointed to the fact that Nolan would say he had to protect his "Aunt."

Lindsey's reaction had been what he had expected but it helped him immensely to hear her voice and her insistence that he back Alex up in her assignment.

Trey now knew that he would insist on his inclusion in the assignment. He had an idea of how to balance his family life with being in Chicago that he would pose to Alex.

When he hung up, he was surprised when Johnnie entered the huddle room. Johnnie told him that he was certain that Alex would take the assignment and he was doing the research to get her the intelligence she would need for the assignment.

He listened and thought about the questions posed by Johnnie. He had come to appreciate Johnnie's investigative skills and his thorough approach to a search effort.

Trey thought about the police friends that had gone to the Chicago police department from when he was on the Minneapolis police force. He gave the names he recalled to Johnnie and promised to call them and find out what they might know.

He felt a surge of apprehension when the Chief waved for him to come into his office.

He listened as the Chief explained that he and Alex had just finished negotiating a deal with the Illinois Lieutenant Governor. He went on to say that he and Alex were to be sworn in as special investigators working directly for the Lieutenant Governor.

He and Alex would receive the minimum of one year's salary that was thirty per cent more than his current one.

The Chief stopped and asked if he was in.

He couldn't say a word and just nodded in the affirmative.

The Chief went on to say that Johnnie would be paid for his investigative efforts in identifying crooked cops.

Trey asked if the sum to be put into the Chief's budget was still intact. The Chief indicated that it was and that their salaries were separate and in addition to that of the original offer.

Trey looked at Alex and commented that he knew never to play poker with her but now he had to give her the title of head negotiator.

He was surprised when the Chief asked if he was ready to be sworn in by the Lieutenant Governor.

This was moving faster than he had expected.

He was glad that he had talked to Lindsey before being called into the office.

Her support made it easy for him to smile and reply that he was ready.

He looked at Alex and said he had one negotiating point before being sworn in.

He said that he wanted weekend live in privileges at her parents' home for Lindsey and Nolan.

He was pleased with Alex's chuckle. She gave him a hug and then said that she would pay for first class tickets for them and throw in fishing trips out on the lake.

He said that in that case he was ready.

The Chief called in Johnnie, Bill, and Travis. He explained that they would be witnesses to the swearing in of Alex and Trey into service in the office of the Illinois Lieutenant Governor's office.

The three of them would give e-signatures to a document in that office.

The Chief then called the Lieutenant Governor.

She commented that she was excited about having the two of them as part of her office staff. She then gave a brief introduction of the witnesses at her end. She made the point that she was one of the witnesses and the Illinois State Reverent, the second witness and would swear them all in.

Trey and Alex raised their right hands and put their left hands on a bible that the Chief was holding. They swore to uphold the laws of the state of Illinois.

The Lieutenant Governor said that she was excited about meeting them both on Monday. They would do lunch and then discuss how Alex planned to proceed.

After the swearing in the Chief hung up.

Trey expected Alex to lead the way out, but she surprised him when she turned to the Chief and let him know that she was planning to go to Chicago on Friday.

The Chief smiled and said that he did not get engaged in her case action decisions and added that she should be careful, but his role now was to make sure she had everything she needed when she needed it.

Trey asked if fishing was included on the weekend and got the response that she would arrange it if he got Nolan and Lindsey to come up.

He listened as Johnnie commented that it was going to be an expensive week for the state of Illinois since he was planning to front load his effort by doing a marathon search for the money trails of bad guys.

He was pleased that the Chief suggested that he and Alex take some time off and make the arrangements that they needed to make.

He wondered what the Chief had in mind when he asked Bill and Travis to stay in the office so they could discuss how they would support the effort.

He learned that Alex had also negotiated their pay from Illinois for any work the two of them did on the case.

Trey walked to his desk a little disoriented.

He looked at Alex and asked if he should be doing anything specific during the week.

She smiled and told him to make sure Lindsey and Nolan were ready for the coming weekend and that taking Nolan fishing would be a wonderful way to start the assignment.

He was unaware of the miracle Johnnie would supply and he also was unaware that Alex would receive protection from the former Cartel wife, now Alex's friend known as the Angel on the hill.

Little did he know that the Mafia would kick off their effort with multiple attacks on their lives only to have their actions take a life elimination boomerang.

7 Mafia Boss

Chicago Mafia Leader Gennaro Visentino was sitting back in his comfortable executive desk chair looking out to Lake Michigan from his fifth-floor corner office. The view reminded him of the view from his family's mountain side home on the outskirts of his Italian hometown overlooking the Tyrrhenian Sea.

The home had been in the family for generations. The one thing that was missing for him in Chicago was the salty fish aroma of the air. The waters of Lake Michigan lacked the fragrance generated by the salt and the kelp of a saltwater sea.

He had not thought about the fact that he missed that smell until he had moved into his new office.

He missed the smells of his mother's cooking and the great food that always graced her table. She was still cooking, and she claimed that cooking for him each time he came home was what was keeping her alive.

He missed Italy, the life style, the food, and his association with his family.

He had not wanted the Chicago assignment but knew not to complain. It was a promotion for his loyalty and his good work.

A no would not have sat well with the Mafia family.

When he took the reins of the Chicago branch, he decided early on that he had to move the Chicago organization to operate more effectively and to generate more income for the family.

He had moved the offices from an old warehouse on the south side of Chicago to the current upscale location on the north side.

He had a long-term lease for the entire fifth floor of the building owned by one of the trucking companies that did much of the movement of the drugs and goods for his organization.

He received praise from the entire Chicago Mafia family.

He groomed his leadership team to run the drug business and operate it like any other successful corporation. The difference from a regular company was that company policies were strictly enforced.

There was an Enforcement VP (EVP), a Collections VP (CVP), a Bribe Management VP (BVP), and a Termination VP (TVP).

The titles described their duties.

Each had several directors that managed the various distribution and collection districts.

The directors managed the actual hands-on operation.

He was pleased when every one of them thanked him for giving them their titles and for the business cards that had raised gold lettering on a black card.

The positions were filled with veteran Mafia personnel. They had risen in the organization by demonstrating their loyalty and their skill.

He was proud of and trusted his current leadership.

His low-key approach in managing the business had paid dividends.

He had widened the influence and the control of the Chicago political scene, and he had eased the police department pressure put on the organization.

A good number of the police facilitated the mafia's business by looking the other way.

He used both honey and vinegar to get cooperation.

The honey was cash in hand given to those that looked away. There were many cops that wanted to remain "honest."

In the old days they would probably have been killed. He instead arranged for them to be moved to districts were there was little business or on walking routes that put them out of the way.

A good number of the police mobile units were receiving enriched mafia honey.

His approach worked and the profit margin went up. He got praise from his leaders in Italy.

He communicated regularly with a top level inside person at the top of the Chicago police department hierarchy.

This person, Jesse Franklin, was second in command and was able to stall or deflect most actions against the business.

The high life lived by that individual bothered him.

He was surprised that the lifestyle had been explained and accepted with a story about it being an inheritance left from his dead parents.

It had worked for many years, so he followed the old adage to "leave what wasn't broken alone."

The attitude and behavior of some of the bad cops bothered him.

There seemed to be a vendetta against Black men and lewd treatment of Black women.

Gennaro knew that the color of his skin was close to being thought of as Black and he was sure that some of the police that he humored thought of him as inferior.

He usually moved the most ardent discriminators to some location where they would not cause trouble. In their cases he would have preferred the old method of eliminating them.

He personally lived quietly in one of the top neighborhoods just outside of the City and was driven in to work each morning.

He and his wife lived a low-profile life but traveled often back to Italy to visit family.

He held dual citizenships but really considered himself Italian and not American.

He loved the time back in Italy and returned as often as possible.

A call from his police informant brought him back from thinking about his next trip to Europe that he and his wife were planning.

The news was bad. Two cops had shot and killed a black man. The black man's family members claimed he was on a beer run and the two cops claimed he was a drug dealer.

Gennaro believed the family. He knew he had two cops that needed reassignment or needed to be thrown under the bus. He let his informant know that the two would not be welcome back and should be moved out of the way.

Then the news got worse.

He was told that the Illinois Lieutenant Governor was trying to make a deal with the City of Cincinnati to get their top detective to come and ferret out bad cops in Chicago.

He asked the name of the detective.

It was a young Black detective, Alex Evercrest, also known as "Cincinnati's Black Annie Oakley," a moniker that she had earned for her deadly accuracy with a gun.

Gennaro had heard of her.

He had followed the news when she had been attacked by the Gulf Drug cartel.

He even believed that she had assassinated its leader, but he had no proof. He personally doubted that any one person could pull of such a feat.

She had become one of the few people in law enforcement that had impressed him.

He did not want her anywhere near Chicago.

He told Jesse to give her a call and to persuade her not to take the job.

If that didn't work, he was to call him back.

He sat and gazed back out to the lake.

He thought for a few moments and then called in his Termination VP.

He asked him to pick out his top two terminators and get them to go to Cincinnati to carry out a hit.

He was certain that this Alex Evercrest would not be warned away.

She would most likely need to be blown away.

He figured he would put his terminators into position and surprise her.

He then called in his support.

She had been with him from the beginning of his time as the Chicago Mafia boss.

She was from his hometown in Italy and often flew back with him.

He asked her to find out the address of Alex Evercrest in Cincinnati.

It was only two hours later that he received another call from Jesse letting him know that the detective had thanked him for the call warning her against accepting the offer from the Illinois Lieutenant Governor and that she was on the way to find him and send him to prison.

It was clear to Gennaro that his informant was nervous. He reassured him that this detective would not make it to Chicago.

He heard a sigh of relieve. He told his informant to go home and relax.

He hung up and called his support about the address and had her share it with his Termination VP.

He walked down to the VP's office and told him to send the terminators to the address and terminate whoever was inside the apartment. They were to fly down immediately, carry out the hit first thing in the morning and then go to the safe house in Texas.

He figured that such a quick reaction would not be expected.

He felt confident that his problems were over.

He went home and spent the evening with his wife planning their next trip to Italy.

They had decided to fly into Amsterdam and take a highspeed train to Rome where they would visit the Vatican. They would then take the train and make several stops on the way to their small hometown in Sicily.

This would be one of their longer trips.

He planned to enjoy both the trip and the food. There was nothing like the food at home and in the small family restaurants where he had grown up.

Tuesday morning, he went into work and waited for the report from his termination VP.

He asked his support to check with the VP to see if he had anything to report.

As he was getting ready to hang up there was a knock at the door.

The expression on the VP's face let him know that he had bad news.

The VP had waited for the call to let him know the hit had occurred.

When it did not come in, he contacted one of the Cincinnati drug distributors and learned that two persons had been shot and killed in the apartment building where Alex Evercrest, the target of the hit, lived.

She had been seen leaving the apartment building and riding off on a bicycle.

Gennaro looked at the VP and said they would need to schedule another hit and that the next time they needed to be successful.

He told him to identify the next two best terminators and let him know that he would determine where the hit would take place.

He arranged for them to meet as soon as he determined where the hit should take place.

He sat and thought about where the best place to make the hit. He wanted a location that would result in the fewest witnesses or casualties. He wanted a place where his victim would not be expecting the hit and where she would be unable to get any sort of help.

The informant he had in the Illinois State Governor's office let him know that Alex and her partner had been sworn in as members of the Lieutenant Governor's office.

This was bad news.

Now the hit would be on an official Illinois employee of the Lieutenant Governor's staff.

He would get lots of heat when he eliminated her.

He also learned that this Alex would be coming to Chicago on the coming Friday and would meet with the Chief of Police and his leadership team that afternoon.

The meeting provided Gennaro with the location where the hit would take place. It was a location that he could arrange for no police to be present.

He asked his support to find out what flight and what time Alex would be arriving to Chicago.

He was not sure how she would do this, but she seemed to be able to reach out and get information from other support functions that always surprised him.

A few hours later she came in with the flight number and time when Alex would arrive.

After thanking her and asking if she wanted to accompany he and his wife on their upcoming a trip home, he decided to call Jesse and set up the hit zone.

Jesse at first objected to the location.

Gennaro said it would be in front of the police station or it could be in the Jesse's office.

He could choose.

Gennaro hung up and called in the terminator VP and had him arrange for the two hit men to be parked across the street from the main entrance to the police station. They were to make the hit of the black female that stepped out of the taxi.

He felt confident that the location was one where no one would expect a hit to take place. He envisioned it being over in seconds and his terminators away from the scene before any police made their appearance.

Gennaro's estimate of being over in seconds was correct.

He was wrong about who would be leaving the scene.

8: *Warm of Heart*

Matt looked out on the river then looked back to the proposal from the Illinois Lieutenant Governor. He contemplated the road ahead in his personal relationship with a woman that took his breath away each time he saw her.

From the very first time, and every time she generated an inner glow in his mind that mesmerized and enthralled him. He had known the very first time he had seen her that she was the one he had waited for all his life.

He worried about her well-being.

Several times he and his EMT unit had been on the scene where she had shot a person or had been shot.

He always listened to the rescue calls in fear of her being the one that was needing emergency care.

He had learned that she was the product of what he considered a wealthy Black family that lived in an upper class neighborhood.

He was the product of a small rural Mississippi town. His grandparents had been slaves that worked out in the fields.

His parents were dirt poor.

His mother cleaned homes for a handful of white families and his father did odd jobs.

He had been helping them since the time he had entered the Marine Corps. He was still sending them a stipend each month even though they said that they could get along on their monthly social security. He knew that they were frugal, but he also knew that they were enjoying being able to periodically go out for dinner.

They had never gone passed the fifth grade in school.

They insisted that he study hard and pushed him to finish High School. He did well scholastically but it was football that opened the future for him.

He became a star receiver on his high school football team. He and the quarter back were unstoppable. Their on the field bond, transferred itself into a deep off the field lifelong friendship.

They both received recommendations to attend the US Naval Academy from one of the Mississippi states senators. They both earned the rank of Junior Lieutenants in the Marines and ended up commanding units in Iraq and later Afghanistan.

He was awarded a metal for rescuing and saving his best friend and his squad.

After their time in service, they both returned to their hometown. His best friend became the sheriff, and he became an EMT.

Life was good but his social life was minimal. He wished to find his soul mate, but it seemed that it would not happen.

As sheriff, his best friend ended up helping Alex capture two fugitives that were involved in bombing her apartment in Cincinnati.

Alex participated in a raid led by the sheriff and during the raid she shot one of the fugitives.

It was on the transport of the wounded fugitive to the hospital that he met Alex for the first time.

On that transport, he could not take his eyes off of her.

He knew he had met his soul mate.

He could not speak.

He had trouble breathing.

When he arrived at the hospital, he managed to offer to buy her a cup of coffee.

It was a lame offer, and he thought he was going to get rejected.

It seemed like a lifetime before she gave him a radiant smile and said she would like that.

The two of them had just started talking over their coffee when they were attacked by the enraged fugitive who they had just brought in.

She was handcuffed to a bed rail that she used like an axe

Alex's reaction had been lightning fast. She had pushed him out of the way and saved him from having his head smashed in.

She subdued the attacker, and they watched as she was led away. The handcuffed attacker managed to take the revolver of the police officers escorting her out of the cafeteria.

She turned and fired her weapon.

Alex fired once.

The angry fugitive fell as a bullet hole appeared in her forehead. It appeared that she was bowing to Alex who kicked the gun from the fugitive's hand.

Alex's partner who had walked in behind the shooter, commented that she was "Cincinnati's Black Annie Oakley."

That phrase instantly became Alex's moniker.

She left a few days later and he knew that he was going to pursue her. He was not about to miss getting the woman he had waited for all his life to meet.

In the following month he looked for and found a job in Cincinnati.

He moved away from his friends and family so he could continue to somehow make the connection for which he was praying.

He knew that she was the love of his life. He knew that he wanted to spend his life with her.

In Cincinnati he and his EMT team arrived at the shooting site where a vengeful mother and father had tried and almost succeeded in killing her.

Alex had shot and killed their son when he had tried to kill Johnnie who had witnessed the killing of a young woman thrown in front of a semi.

He had stayed with Alex in the emergency room until she woke up. He was holding her hand when her eyes opened.

Her smile warmed his heart.

Her mother, who he had called, was also in the room. She later said that she knew instantly that Alex had found her soul mate.

They had been a pair since then.

He knew he was the support, and she was the lead. For him it was as it should be.

He shook his head and came back to the present and the offer from the Illinois Lieutenant Governor that he was holding in his hand.

A shiver went up his spine.

He knew that she would accept the offer.

He knew that she was using the lunch meeting to establish her support team and to sense their mood.

He looked across the river at Covington and thought about his ability to support her on this case.

His inclusion in the lunch invitation meant that Alex was seeking his opinion and his support.

She would always have his support.

His opinion was that it was a suicide case.

He was surprised and pleased that Bill and Travis, the detective team that often competed with Alex and Trey for recognition, were included at the lunch meeting.

This meant that Alex was seeking all the information and support possible.

Johnnie had called him to let him know where the lunch would be held so Johnnie's presence was no surprise.

Matt knew that Johnnie would take a bullet for Alex, and he would provide her with the invaluable intel.

He felt the least capable to physically support her. He would give his life to protect her, and he would not be present when she encountered the bad guys.

At best he would show up and hope that she was the victor of any gun battle she was in.

He hoped that she thought of him as her emotional support.

He decided that the best way to support her on this case was to arrange weekend trips to her parent's home where he was sure she would be. He talked to his supervisor and made the arrangement to spend weekends in Evanston.

He knew that he would continue to make special arrangements so he would be there for her.

There was no getting around that she was and would always be the strong one in their relationship.

He wanted to be there when she needed him.

When Alex asked him to walk her back to the station, he was elated.

He anticipated her invitation to visit on the weekends and go fishing.

He listened as she explained that she was thinking about taking the assignment.

If she decided to take it, she would ask to be sworn in as a special agent to the Illinois Lieutenant Governor's office.

She let him know that Trey would be with her on the assignment.

She explained that she planned to ask for more from the State of Illinois.

As they rounded the corner and came to the front of the Cincinnati Library Alex stopped. She asked if he remembered when only a few months ago his EMT team had arrived at the scene of the gun battle she had been in, and he had seen the planner of the shooting standing a block away.

She shared that a hand from above had saved her that day and he had been key in identifying the person who had planned the shooting.

She went on to say that she was always looking for the hand from above and she was always looking at him for his support.

The phone rang. He knew that she would normally have ignored it but this time she answered.

She put the phone into speaker mode so he could hear the conversation.

It was a threat of violence to her and those around her.

He knew immediately that the call would crystalize Alex's decision to accept the offer.

She thanked the caller for helping her make her decision and hung up.

He stopped her when she started to apologize for taking the call.

He gave her a hug and said he would support her no matter what.

He let her know that he would arrange to be there every weekend during her special assignment.

He was about to learn the speed at which events would transpire and the actions he would take that would raise the hair on the back of his neck.

9 Angel on the Hill

*B*ill looked across the river to Covington but what was on his mind was the impossible assignment that Alex was being offered.

He was well aware of the corruption in the Chicago Police department. It was what he mildly thought of as bad. He had acquaintances that had shared many of the internal details and what was shared was of an organization that had rot and mold on the organizations roots and had spoiling hanging fruit on the main branches of the organization.

He wondered how anyone could possibly come in and cure the cancer.

The power and involvement of the Mafia was another main concern for him.

He knew that they were responsible for much of the corruption. The spoiling fruit basically worked for them.

He thought back at how the Cincinnati Detective department had changed. He had wanted the promotion to be Chief but had been turned down.

He figured it was because there was a push to integrate the detective unit, and the person selected was a very qualified individual and he was black.

Bill had contemplated retiring, but he enjoyed the work. He could not envision himself, fishing or golfing or doing anything else. He decided to help the new Chief to make the department a better place.

When he took on this supportive role, he became sensitized to the bias and discrimination of many of the white police officers.

It was eye opening for him because in the past he had not recognized the bias of the other folks. He did not feel the same about the color of a person's skin as it became so apparent to him after the new Black Chief got in place.

Color to him had little to do with their character, honesty, or capability.

When the Chief recruited and hired Alex, Bill once again was made aware of the color barrier when it became clear that no one was willing to be her back up partner.

It was a promotion for whoever took the backup position.

Bill thought it weird that even promotion and increased pay was not enough. The problem was that the white police officers were rejecting the role because she was a young black woman. He shook his head about the two types of discrimination.

He let the Chief know that he was willing to be the junior backup partner. The Chief thanked him but let him know that he was too valuable to put in that position and that he would look for someone outside of the city.

Bill was impressed when he met Trey, a tall blue eyed, ramrod straight ex-Marine. The Chief introduced him and highlighted the fact that Trey had received a purple heart and had received another metal for his bravery in single handedly saving his buddy's platoon from a battle where they were pinned down by the enemy.

He and Travis had gone from being skeptical of Alex's and Trey's capabilities to being ardent supporters of their efforts.

He watched as her personality and friendliness transformed the work environment from one of rivalry to one that embraced supporting each other.

Work became more enjoyable than before.

His decision to stay had been rewarded.

He and Travis would do all they could to help but they would be more like spectators sitting in the colosseum watching the gladiators battle it out between themselves.

He looked at Travis and recognized the look of concern on his face. He was sure the Travis would be having thoughts similar to his.

They would do all they could to help but what they needed was help from above.

That thought immediately made him think of "The Angel on the hill."

She might have the connections and be able to call off the Mafia.

He would surface that idea later when he was working with Johnnie.

After lunch, he and Trevor discussed the situation. The two of them went into a huddle room and noodled how they might be able to help.

They both knew cops in the Chicago police department that they considered honest. They agreed to call them and see what they could learn.

Bill shared his idea about contacting Alex's friends in Mexico. Travis suggested that they should also call Harold Zimmerman in the DEA's office in Chicago and let him know about the offer Alex had received from the Illinois Lieutenant Governor.

He was certain Harold would do what he could to help.

They stopped and went to the coffee area and got two bottles of water to take to their desks.

He saw that Trey and Johnnie were sitting at their desks.

Alex was not at her desk, so he figured she was still walking back from the restaurant.

Bill raised his water bottle and gave the salute to "one of the most dangerous assignments that he would never take."

Trey shook his head and instead raised his coffee cup and replied, "to the assignment that Alex and he would blow out of the water."

Bill raised his water bottle and said, "here, here we will all cheer."

He looked over to see the Chief standing in his office doorway raising his coffee cup in agreement.

Alex appeared as if on que.

He was not surprised to see her walk directly into the Chief's office and close the door. The window blinds went down.

He looked around and asked if anyone wanted to be a fly on the wall and listen what was being said.

He watched Trey walk into one of the huddle rooms and make a call.

He was sure that his wife, Lindsey, would be on the other end The call did not last long.

He had noted that Trey shook his head in agreement to whatever Lindsey was saying.

He then watched as Johnnie went into the huddle room with his computer and seemed to be making notes.

He looked over at Trevor and said that they should make sure to give Johnnie the names to their contacts. He hoped his friends would be able to identify some of the bad apples.

As Trey walked out of the huddle room, the door to the Chief's office opened and Alex waved Trey over.

Bill knew that Trey had become part of the package.

He hoped that Lindsey had agreed to the situation that was unfolding.

He asked Trevor what he thought might be going on in the office and agreed with him that Alex was bringing Trey up to speed on what she had so far negotiated and asking if Trey agreed.

Not long after the Chief opened the door and waved all three of them to come into his office.

He, Trevor, and Johnnie listened as the Chief explained that their role would be witnesses to Alex and Trey being sworn in as special agents for the Illinois Lieutenant Governor's office.

Bill could not wait to learn what Alex might have negotiated.

What he was oblivious to was that his connection to an Angel on the Hill, would profoundly change the nature of Alex's assignment.

10 Dual Concerns

*T*he week had started out bad for Jesse and the bad seemed to be accelerating downhill. He felt like a mogul skier that had lost control and would have a serious fall at any moment.

He had two, "bad cops" that had gone rogue and out of control.

He was also concerned about the information from his contact at the office of the Illinois Lieutenant Governor that she was arranging to bring in a special investigator to root out bad cops from the Chicago Police department.

He chuckled to himself that he was the top bad cop on the force who worked for a political boss that was clueless about what was going on. He knew that he was running the shop.

Having the detective being brought into the Lieutenant Governor's staff was to him a huge mogul that he would need to surmount if he wanted to come out of it on top.

He knew how to handle the first problem. He was going to put the two out to pasture, be run over by the bus or suggest they go elsewhere.

As soon as elsewhere crossed his mind he decided to let them know that they should seek employment in some other city while they were still able to do so.

He wanted them gone and out of his hair. He was sure they had killed an innocent man just because he was black and had been at the wrong place at the wrong time.

The two were no longer of any use to him.

The news from the Lieutenant Governor's office concerned him more. He went for his secure call protocol walk outside and called Gennaro, the Chicago Mafia Boss, and let him know of the situation.

He was surprised that Gennaro knew the name of the black detective being brought in for the special investigation.

He listened as he was told to call the detective and persuade her not to take the job. He was instructed to make the call immediately and report back on the reply that he received. He was to make sure that she understood she would get no help from any individual in the Chicago police department and there would be a huge risk to her and her family.

He took out his frustration by crushing his throwaway phone with the heel of his shoe. He threw the pieces into the sidewalk waste container.

He was now thinking about the words to use when he made the call. He stopped by the coffee pot and got himself a fresh cup.

He needed a boost.

He was not comfortable about making the call but did because he could not relegate it to anyone else.

He realized that his frustration had cost him a throwaway phone. He got another throwaway phone, went for another walk, and made the call.

He was surprised at the pleasant voice on the other end. She did not sound anything like he had been expecting.

He used a deep tone to warn her not to take the role being offered by the Illinois Lieutenant Governor. He made the point that her life and the lives of those she loved would be in great jeopardy since there might be collateral damage if she accepted.

He was not expecting the answer he received.

She thanked him for being the catalyst that had just helped her decide to accept the case and that she would be talking to him very soon.

She gave a small laugh and said the that his use of a throw away phone would not help and that she would have his name before she left Cincinnati.

She then hung up on him before he could respond.

It was clear he had not successfully cleared the mogul and was about to crash into the next one.

He did not know how he was going to handle the situation.

He thought through the conversation.

This time he used the same throw away to call Gennaro and let him know that the call to warn off the Cincinnati detective had not been successful and that they had a problem on their hands.

Gennaro assured him that she would be dealt with and that she was no longer his worry. He should focus on his roque cops and deal with them.

As Jesse's foot came down on the throwaway phone, he wondered how she knew that he was using one.

The next order of business was to clear out the two rogue cops.

He planned to interrogate them, but he first turned the television on and played back the news reports on the shooting on the young black man. All the channels had a report of the shooting of a local drug dealer that had resisted arrest. His conversation with the coroner earlier at the crime scene led him to believe that the driver was shot while still in the car.

The coroner's preliminary report that had been placed on his desk indicated that the downward angle of the shots confirmed the initial on-site assessment.

He had the two rogue cops called into his office. Once they were seated, he asked them to tell him what had happened. He had helped fabricate many cover stories and immediately knew he was listening to a very bad one. They had the driver of the car getting out and drawing a weapon before they both shot him.

He figured they at least should have read the coroner's report.

He let them know that they should use the two weeks of desk duty to look outside of Chicago for another job and if they stayed, he would have them walking some back water neighborhood for the rest of their time on the force.

He informed them that internal investigation unit had started interviewing and seeking answers to the shooting.

It was clear to him that if they decided to stay, he would sacrifice them to keep control of the rest of his kingdom.

He felt as if he were in a pressure cooker. It was whistling and the pressure cooker weight rocking back and forth to regulate the pressure was about to be blown off.

He knew that he had to do something to relieve the stress.

He decided that he should take a vacation to his condo in Florida.

He called his wife and asked her if she felt like spending a few days walking on the beach. He had purchased the condo because it had a great view of the gulf and there was a long white sand beach that ran for miles.

It was a place of calm where he often went when he felt too much pressure at work.

Too much pressure was what he now felt.

He suggested the weekend after the upcoming one. She agreed and his mind took him for a stroll along his favorite stretch of beach.

It was good that he took that mental stroll while he could. He would later take many similar strolls but only in his mind. His days were numbered, and the number of days was low.

He was about to meet a much better mogul skier.

11 The Price of Fame

*T*he support she received from those in the Cincinnati detective unit made coming to work enjoyable.

She had grown very close to Johnnie a Vietnam war veteran who had a magic touch in mining data bases.

Her work partner, Trey, was a decorated Iraq war veteran. He and his wife, Lindsey and their son Nolan had become her family. Nolan called her Aunt Alex and for that he always got a treat from her.

The competing detective team of Bill and Trevor had transitioned from competitors to collaborators.

The Cincinnati detective unit had become a great place to work.

The very generous financial offer from the Illinois Lieutenant Governor for her services to root out the bad Chicago police officers had impressed her, but she was unsure if she should accept it.

The fact that it would be dangerous was obvious but the effect it might have on her personal relationship was what was of a bigger concern to her.

Her current relationship to Matt was the most important aspect of her life.

She had listened to everyone's opinion during lunch, and they had been a consistent with a message of "you must be crazy to consider it."

She walked back with Matt talking about the situation.

His position would be the deciding piece of the decision puzzle.

She listened to his suggestion that he come up on weekends and the two of them could go fishing, walk the beach, sit by the pool, and enjoy margaritas.

She stopped and gave him a hug and kiss.

He always had a way to capture her heart.

As if on que her phone rang. Normally she would not have answered but she had a feeling that the call might have to do with the offer.

She put her phone in speaker mode and answered in her normal, "Hello, hope all is well with you."

She stopped walking when it became clear that she was being threatened. The caller warned her not to take the role being offered by the Illinois Lieutenant Governor.

She replied that the call had just catalyzed her decision to accept the role, but she was upping the requirement so that she would have the authority to arrest and prosecute any corrupt cop she uncovered.

She then said that she would see him very soon and she would have enough on him to make sure he would spend the next twenty years in prison.

She then said, "Have a good day" and hung up.

Matt had heard the threat; she listened as he reiterated his support for her.

She looked at him and said that he had helped her overcome her worry about the effect that the assignment would have on their relationship.

She then smiled and told him she looked forward to going out fishing with him on weekends.

She waved her phone in the air and said that the caller was the catalyst to push her over the decision hump.

She was now certain that she would take on the assignment if the Illinois Lieutenant Governor was willing to accept some additional terms of employment and costs.

She told Matt that she intended to ask that she and Trey be full employees of the Lieutenant Governor's office and that no matter how quickly they resolved the problem, they were guaranteed one year's salary. Their salary was to be separate from the money that had been promised to the Cincinnati Detective Department.

Her current Cincinnati salary would not be used. She wanted to ensure that the Chief was able to hire the two additional detective teams he had been requesting.

She took Matt's arm and walked on past the Library and then two blocks later turned toward the station.

Matt had let her know that he had arranged for his team to pick him up in the station parking lot. She saw them standing and waiting for him.

Alex gave him a hug and suggested that he come by when his shift ended or for breakfast if his shift ran late into the night.

He suggested breakfast.

Alex walked into the station. She went straight to the Chief's office and closed the door.

The Chief looked at her and smiled.

He knew the look.

He got up closed the blinds and asked if she was ready to talk to Lieutenant Governor Stradford.

Alex responded by nodding and saying, "make the call but I have some requests that must be met for me to accept the job. One request is for me and Trey, one is for you and one if for Johnnie."

She then stated that she and Trey would need to have the authority to arrest those they identified as bad cops.

They would also be on the Lieutenant Governor's payroll with a thirty percent pay raise and a one-year salary promise even if the task was accomplished faster.

Johnnie would also be part of the package but would remain in Cincinnati. He would be available to her as her sleuth analyst.

He was to get as high of a pay raise that the Chief could arrange.

She continued and said that the dollar amount promised to the Cincinnati Detectives department would be the amount in the document sent to Cincinnati by the Illinois Lieutenant Governor.

She looked at the Chief and stated that Trey's and her current pay would be put back into the department's budget for the duration of one year.

She knew by the look on his face that the Chief liked what he heard.

He said they should call and see if the Lieutenant Governor was still interested.

He commented that he would keep in mind that she would be more expensive when she returned to his payroll.

When he got on the phone, he let the Lieutenant Governor know that he had her on speaker phone and that Alex was on the line with him.

She immediately said they should call her Jane and that she was the only one at her end. She said hello to Alex and reminded her that the last time the two of them had seen each other was at Alex's high school graduation party at her parent's house.

Alex replied that it had been too long and that she remembered that party very well and that Jane had worn a bright red dress, matching high heel shoes, and a yellow rose in her hair.

Alex commented that every person in the room had made a point of how gorgeous she looked.

Jane laughed and said that she would have to look at pictures to see how accurate Alex's memory was.

Then the Chief said that he had some addendums to the request that had been sent to his office.

He repeated what Alex had said but stated it as if it was his requirement.

There was silence on the other end that was long enough for the Chief to raise his eyebrows in a questioning gesture.

Jane finally responded and said that she bet that Alex had come up with those requirements. It sounded a lot like her mother's tough bargaining tactics.

She said she hesitated so that she had time to ask her support if there was enough money in the budget to cover the request. Her support said they could only cover the amount if it was split into six months this year and six months in the next fiscal.

Alex responded that the commitment to the condition of including her current partner and that they have the authority to arrest was more important than the timing of the cash flow.

Jane chuckled and said she was now sure she was talking to Alex's mother. She said that she had not bargained for two individuals but understood Alex's request to have her current partner be part of the package.

She said that giving Alex the authority to arrest would be part of the role.

She asked if the Chief's support would work the money side with her support.

She then asked if Alex and her partner were ready to be sworn in as officer's reporting to her organization.

Alex replied that she was and that her Cincinnati detective partners would all be supporting her.

She commented that Jane was getting a great deal, and the results would exceed her expectations.

The Chief suggested they keep the line open but take a moment so that he could call in Trey and the folks that would act as witnesses to the swearing in.

Jane said that was appropriate because she needed to do the same.

Alex went to the door and waved Trey in and pointed to Johnnie, Bill, and Trevor to come to the office.

The Chief explained the situation and the witnessing role.

The swearing in ceremony went smoothly and was over very quickly.

Jane asked when her two new employees would report to work.

Alex said that they would be in Chicago on Friday and that she would like to have an initial meeting with the Chief of Police at three that afternoon.

Jane replied that she would have to get use to the speed at which Alex moved.

She thanked Jane when she said that she would have her support arrange for the meeting.

Jane asked if she could meet both of them on Monday in her office.

She and Trey accepted, and the call ended.

Alex looked around the room and said that she knew she would need the help of all of them. She said that she understood that she was walking into a den of angry lions.

She went on to say that it was their role to see that she walked out in one piece.

She shared the fact that she had already received a threat on her life as well as those around her if she took the assignment. She suggested that they all take extra precautions to be safe.

She looked at Johnnie and let him know that she had negotiated for his services and that he was getting the highest pay raise that the Chief could arrange.

She told him she was going to need all the miracles that he could generate.

The first miracle was to identify who at the top of the Chicago police hierarchy was corrupt. She said that she thought he had been the one to threaten her and she wanted to confront him on her first visit.

She laughed when Trevor complained that he hadn't received a pay raise in years and asked if Alex would put in a good word for him.

The Chief stepped in and said they should all get back to work.

Alex led the way out to her desk and sat down. She looked over at Bill and asked what he thought about the assignment and her arrangements.

She nodded when he said that he agreed with her that they should all watch their backs. He went on to say that moving fast was a great idea and if Johnnie did identify the top guy, she should take him out immediately. He then pointed out that the top guy was probably connected to the mafia and that would pose an additional threat.

The Chief came out of his office and let Alex know that his support had made the flight reservations to Chicago for one on Friday.

He then commented that the events of the day had exhausted him, and he was calling it a day and suggested they all take the rest of the day off.

Alex thanked him and said she was going to get on the treadmill and run until she dropped.

Everyone took the recommendation.

She and Johnnie rode their bikes back to their apartment building.

Johnnie promised her that he would have a list of who the bad guys were from top to bottom.

The next day the smell of coffee woke her up at five thirty. She rose and dished out her yogurt, honey and nuts bowl and poured a cup of coffee. She was standing at the counter in the center of the kitchen area. Her weapon was within hands reach.

She looked at the chair propped at an angle under the doorknob. She must have done it reflexively the night before because she could not remember doing it. She was about to step around to remove it when there was a knock on the door.

She knew it was not Johnnie who knocked to the rhythm of "a shave and a haircut" and Matt always used a flat palm knock. She picked up her weapon and stepped up on the stool that was to the side of the door. With her foot she kicked the chair from under the doorknob and unlocked the door.

Her gun was in hand her left hand. She called out, "come on in, the door is unlocked."

She watched as the door handle turned, and the door was kicked open. The roar of a shot gun being fired following the kick reverberated loudly in the apartment.

She reflexively shot the assailant in the side of the head. As he was falling, she shot the second attacker between the eyes. The second shooters shotgun went off and shot his accomplice in the back. She put a second shot into the person in back as he went down.

She looked down at the bloody mess on the floor.

She looked at the dent in the door and knew that Johnnie would complain that she went through too many apartments and too many doors.

She made sure there was not another shooter and verified that the two attackers were dead. She then called the station for backup.

She took a stand in the hallway. When Johnnie came out of the elevator, she called to him to let him know she was OK. Her next-door neighbor looked out and Alex let her know that things were in control and that she would come over later to let her know what had happened but that for now she should stay in her apartment.

She gave a small laugh when as she expected Johnnie complained that he would have to replace her door for the third time.

She gave him a hug and apologized for her rude guests.

The police responders soon dominated the hallway. She let them know that she would be going into the station.

The lead police officer on the scene started to object but Alex held up her hand and told him to call her Chief with his objections.

She turned in her gun as evidence and then asked him to get one of the other officers to lift her bike out of the apartment.

With Johnnie in the lead, she rode in. On the way she thought about how quickly the attack had occurred. The warning had been serious and the people in Chicago were determined to keep her away.

She instructed Johnnie to see if he could identify for whom the two dead shooters worked.

She smiled when Johnnie bargained with her for her cookies if he were successful.

She promised him trays of cookies for all the miracles he could deliver and would need to continue to deliver. She let him know that she needed them all.

She commented that the attack seemed to be something that the Chicago PD would not do.

She suspected that the Mafia had been activated.

Alex called her mother and warned her to take extra precaution. She let her mother know of the attack and suggested that her mother get security upgraded.

She commented that security should take the attitude that the attackers would shoot first.

Alex listened as her mother tried to apologize for having gotten her involved in the corruption issue in the Chicago legal system.

Alex let her know that she was already on the payroll of the Illinois Lieutenant Governor and that she planned to be at home Friday afternoon and that Trey would be staying at the house as well.

Her mother said that she would take precaution at the office and that she would prepare something good for a Friday evening dinner.

Alex suggested something light and easy. She asked her mother to warn her father about adding security at his office.

After hanging up she called Harold Zimmerman with the DEA and filled him in on her situation.

Over the span of several cases, the two of them had become good friends.

She asked if he would check up on her parents.

Alex was unaware that her positive attitude and behavior had resulted in very loyal and supportive friends.

They were friends that leaned in and moved toward the danger.

12 No Brainer

*T*rey took the Chief's suggestion to go home. He sent a text to Lindsey letting her know that he would be home early.

As he drove, he was going over the fact that Alex was the person that had helped him overcome most of his PTSD. She seemed to know how to draw him out and away from the dark cloud that often darkened his thinking.

Lindsey had commented that she saw a noticeable improvement in him since he had taken the job and worked with Alex.

Alex had gotten him into AA and helped him stay sober. She shared the fact that she had joined while she was in college when she realized that she had lost control.

She had saved his life multiple times. He would always try to be where he could back her up.

He knew that Lindsey was going to be as supportive as he was. He was worried about the assignment having a negative effect on Nolan.

When he got home, he mentioned his concern to her.

Lindsey had made her favorite tea and had some snacks prepared. She suggested that they talk about how to handle the situation.

She took Nolan to his room and got him started doing his homework.

As an incentive to Nolan, she said that she would make him his favorite pizza for dinner.

She returned to the kitchen and poured both of them a cup. She then asked to hear more about the upcoming assignment.

Trey sat down and took a bite of a raisin oatmeal cookie. He complemented her on how good it tasted.

She smiled and told him not to try to divert the discussion.

He then shared that he was now officially working for the Lieutenant Governor of Illinois and had received a thirty percent increase in his pay.

He gave a small laugh, said that Alex had gotten that for both of them and she had also made sure that Johnnie got a raise as well.

Lindsey marveled at the negotiation skill that Alex had demonstrated, and she commented on the fact that Alex had given him every opportunity not to be part of the assignment.

He saw the look of concern as she asked if it was so dangerous that the state of Illinois was willing to pay them so much.

He replied that it was going to be one of the more dangerous cases that he and Alex had undertaken but he reminded Lindsey that every case that they had been on had involved great danger.

He added that the entire Cincinnati Detective unit thought it was extremely dangerous.

He said if Lindsey objected, he would not go.

Lindsey shook her head negatively and said that he had to go. Alex was family and she had risked her life to save him and to avenge the beating that the Gulf cartel lackeys had given him.

It was a no brainer.

He had to go.

Her concern was that Nolan needed his dad and wondered how to handle that situation.

Trey replied that Alex had given him an open invitation to have her and Nolan visit whenever they could.

He added that Alex had suggested starting this weekend and had already purchased two first class seats on the Friday afternoon flight and that Alex had arranged for her Chicago driver to pick them up at the luggage area.

Lindsey commented that Alex was indeed more than a work partner, she was family.

The discussion ended when Nolan came in and said that he was done with his homework and was ready for pizza.

The next morning Trey answered the phone and heard Alex say that she was standing in the hallway outside her apartment over two dead men who had tried to kill her.

She told him to stay with Lindsey and Nolan and be prepared in case he was attacked.

Trey took down his weapon from the elevated storage location and put it on. He told Lindsey to make sure the doors were locked. He placed chairs under both door handles.

When Nolan asked what was going on, he told him that Aunt Alex had asked him to make sure the doors were locked. She said he should stay home from school and enjoy a free day.

Nolan looked at them and said, "Aunt Alex would only say that if bad guys were going to do something bad."

Trey smiled and said that he had guessed right and that his aunt was watching out for them.

He let Nolan know about his assignment and the fact that he would be in Chicago during the week but that on weekends he would either come back to Cincinnati to be home or Nolan would come to Alex's house for the weekend.

The last part excited Nolan. He said he wanted to go as often as possible and that he also wanted to go fishing with Aunt Alex.

Trey and Lindsey looked at each other and knew that Nolan would get spoiled during this assignment.

Lindsey looked at him and said that their worry about their child was not going to be an issue. The issue would be how spoiled he might become.

A short time later Alex called again and said that she would be over at noon to discuss security for Lindsey and Nolan. She let him know that Sheriff Williams would also be there.

He and the Sheriff had shared many cups of coffee in their favorite Loveland coffee shop since the Sheriff and he and Alex had solved the case of the long missing Annie Scotts.

Annie was rescued from the woods of Pennsylvania. She had two daughters, Linda and Lorie that now were best friends with Nolan.

The two girls both referred to Alex as "Aunt Alex."

Annie was now a very successful and wealthy artist. She credited Alex with launching her career as a professional artist.

That case had made it clear to him that all cases were personal and that the idea of separation of work and home was a hard one to make happen.

Trey suggested to Alex that he prepare lunch, and they could all discuss the security situation then when she got to his house.

Trey was used to the speed at which events roiled around Alex as she plowed swiftly ahead but he was not prepared for what was about to happen.

He was pleased that Alex had gotten Sheriff Williams to provide extra security during the time they were in Chicago.

He had no idea that Bill, Trevor, and Johnnie would secure the aid of the "Angel on the hill" to protect Alex and that protection would be delivered by the Greek goddesses the Furies who delivered vengeance and retribution to punish men for their crimes.

13 The Good, The Maybe and The Bad

When the swearing ceremony was over, Bill and Trevor looked at each other as Johnnie asked them if they had ever heard of a Cincinnati detective being sought after by any state's Lieutenant Governor.

Before either of them could answer, the Chief asked the three of them to stay in the office. He looked at them and said he was putting all three of them on one team. Their job was to provide Alex with all the intel that they could develop. They would only get another case when they had exhausted their ability to get more intel on the Chicago situation.

The Chief told them that even though they didn't deserve it he was getting all three of them the best pay raise he could arrange but they needed to have Alex's and Trey's backs.

Bill responded that even with no pay raise he knew that all three of them would do all that was in their power to help.

He said that he planned to take the lead in getting a thorough information search implemented.

The Chief thanked him and said he knew that the three of them would give it their all. He said that he might have some information that might be useful.

The three of them left the office and Bill suggested they hold a meeting in one of the huddle rooms and develop a plan.

Trevor looked at Johnnie and commented that Bill always tried to be the boss but that he was looking to Johnnie to discover the bad guys.

Bill appreciated Johnnie's reply that he always worked better when someone else took care of developing and managing a plan. His expertise was to tease information from databases and the web. He hated to do the organizing. Johnnie said he always lost his way and needed someone to bring him back to the trail.

Trevor replied that Johnnie didn't have to fan the fires of Bill's ego because his ego was large enough.

Bill laughed and replied that it would not be the fires of any one's ego that would burn but the fires under their collective butts if they failed to get the intel that Alex needed.

Bill used the white board and wrote down,

Good Guys,

Maybe Bad Guys,

Bad Guys.

He drew lines down so there were three columns. He then said that he knew some of the Good Guys and some Maybe Bad Guys but did not have any names for the Bad Guys column.

He suggested that when they get done, they ask the Chief to look at the list and see if he had any names to add.

He was about to go on when there was a tap on the window. He turned to see Trey standing looking in.

He waved Trey in.

Trey said he was walking by getting ready to leave when he saw the three columns. He said that he had two names for the good guy's column and one for the maybe bad guy's column.

He gave the names and then said he was taking the Chief's advice and going home.

Bill said they were taking the Chief's advice and working on keeping the pay raise the Chief had promised them.

Bill thanked Trey and then watched him walk out.

Once the door closed, he commented that he was glad that Alex had a steel backed boned person like Trey as a partner.

He turned back to the list and said he had one for the good guy's column and three names for the maybe bad guy's column.

He looked at Trevor and took down the names that he had.

He then walked to the Chief's office and returned with the Chief.

He watched as the Chief reviewed what was on the white board.

The Chief gave him two names. One on the Good Guy's column and one in the Bad Guy's column.

It was the first name on the Bad Guy's column.

Bill asked him to explain the one in the Bad Guy's column. The name had surprised him because it was the name of the Chicago Police Department Deputy Chief.

This was the second in command of the force and the one that actually ran the department.

He listened as the Chief explained that years ago, the Deputy Chief had been asked to leave the police department in which they both worked. The person who was now the Chicago Police Deputy Chief was accused of planting drugs and a gun on an innocent man. That was many years ago and maybe he had changed his stripes but most likely he had learned to hide his crooked actions better and was getting away with it.

Johnnie chuckled and said he already had uncovered dirt to support the Chief's theory about stripes. The deputy had more wealth than any Deputy Chief could possibly earn legally.

The Deputy Chief lived in a luxury condo; he had a large yacht harbored in Chicago and a condo in Florida.

All the property was under his wife's name.

He wondered how the state had not already exposed him. Johnnie commented that there must be some powerful person that was shielding him.

Bill chuckled when Johnnie suggested that the Chief get Alex to arrange a raise for himself.

He pointed out that he had just provided Alex with the head of the snake.

Bill thanked the Chief and after he left, he said that the only explanation was that the Mafia was providing political protection to the Chicago Deputy Police Chief.

He listened as Trevor conjectured that they should get a message to "The Angel on the Hill" about the situation.

Johnnie spoke up and said he would send a message to the Angel's brother, Adolfo. He and Adolfo had collaborated before and had a very good relationship.

A few moments later he got a response from Adolfo. Johnnie explained the situation and asked if Adolfo could be of help.

Adolfo replied that he would work with the Angel. He shared that he knew that the Gulf Cartel and the Chicago mafia were butting heads.

He would see about the cartel giving the Chicago Mafia a hands-off warning ultimatum about Alex and Trey.

Adolfo called back a short time later and shared that a warning would come from the current Gulf Cartel Leadership and be given directly to the Chicago Mafia Boss.

There would be no room for misinterpretation about the ultimatum.

He pointed out that the Mafia knew that the Cartel had people in place in Chicago that could enforce the warning, and it would most likely heed the warning.

Johnnie thanked Adolfo and told him that he owed him another bottle of his favorite wine.

Bill looked at Johnnie with added respect.

He complimented him on his ability to provide Alex backup by a drug cartel.

He had never heard of a cop getting back up from a drug cartel.

This was a first for him.

He looked at Trevor and asked him if he had ever heard of such a thing.

Trevor shook his head and said that they should all go, down a cold one and then go home.

Johnnie invited them to his apartment for the cold one. He said he wanted to continue to mine the data bases and get the material ready to give to Alex before she left for Chicago. He planned on working through the night if the mining was good.

Bill and Trevor took him up on the offer. Trevor agreed that they should front load their effort so that Alex would have as much information as possible.

He called home to let wife know that he was working late.

Bill knew that both he and Trevor wanted to learn what Johnnie was likely to find.

He had no idea how significant the information the three of them gathered would prove to be.

It would save both Alex and Trey.

14 Kidnapped

Alex used Wednesday and Thursday to think through how to approach rooting out bad cops. She had agreed with Trey to work from home and interact on their computers.

She replied in the positive when Trey suggested they have dinner at his house on Thursday evening.

He invited Matt as well.

She was pleased with the invitation. Since it would give her a place to be other than her apartment. She had been lucky that the assassins had been using slugs in their shot guns. The only damage were the three shattered windows and the dent in the door when it had been kicked in.

When she and Matt arrived, Nolan came running to them and gave them both hugs.

Then he blurted out that he had been promised weekend trips to Alex's mom's house while she and his dad took out the bad guys in Chicago.

Trey laughed and said that the beans had been spilled and now Alex knew how he had negotiated being her backup.

Alex smiled and replied that it would be great to see Nolan every weekend.

Lindsey said that it would be at least twenty minutes before dinner was ready and everyone should get something to drink and get comfortable.

Matt asked Nolan if he had any games they could play while they waited for what he was sure would be a great dinner.

Nolan took his hand and led the way to his bedroom.

Lindsey signaled for Alex to follow her into the kitchen.

There she told Alex that there had never been a question about Trey backing her up and that she would have insisted if he had hesitated.

She shared that both of them had worried about Nolan's reaction to his dad being away during the weekdays but when he learned he would spend the weekend at Alex's mother's home he was really excited.

Alex thanked Lindsey for letting her know.

She said she would understand if later they had to change their minds. She did not want the assignment to negatively affect Nolan.

Lindsey gave a small laugh and said there would be no mind changing later and she was hoping that Nolan didn't get too spoiled by Alex's parents who he now considered his third set of grandparents.

Later during dinner, Alex looked across the table at the stir-fried mix of vegetables and sliced beef served over brown rice with several stalks of asparagus on the side that provided a green border.

A separate small side salad completed the setting.

She complimented Lindsey on the dinner.

Nolan was the leader of the conversation as he asked about going fishing and if it was still warm enough to swim in the pool. It was clear that to him the assignment meant he was going to get mini vacations on weekends.

Alex made a point that all tickets to Chicago were her treat as well as the rides to her house.

She let Nolan know that the pool was heated.

Lindsey suggested that they did not need to have first class seats.

Alex waved that fact aside and said she would make Trey drink water instead of drinking beer with her dad.

Matt asked if he could get the same first class deal that Nolan was getting.

Nolan spoke up and agreed that Matt should get the same deal.

Alex laughed and asked if Matt had bribed him to agree.

Nolan shook his head but repeated that the deal should be the same.

Alex bent her head and replied that then she had no choice but to get him first class tickets as well and that she would have to start drinking water with his dad.

Once dinner was over, Alex thanked Lindsey for having both her and Matt over.

She let Trey know that she would likely be late coming in the next mornings and that he should take his time.

They had a flight at one and she wanted to get to the airport at least an hour earlier.

Alex then led the way to the waiting taxi. She asked Matt about the rest of the evening, and he let her know that he had traded time with one of his co-workers so he could get the weekend off and would be on duty as soon as he got back to the fire station. He said he would let her know about the weekend after he had a chance to talk to his bosses.

The crime scene had been cleared, and she noticed that Johnnie had already boarded the window and had replaced the door.

She changed into her running clothes and took the elevator down. She went to Johnnie's apartment and used their common door knock.

When the door opened, Alex took in the fact that both Bill and Travis were sitting at the dining room table.

Johnnie said that he would invite her in, but he, Bill, and Travis were busy working on a special gift for her.

Alex replied that she could hardly wait, said she was going for a run and then she was calling it a night.

She looked at Bill and Travis and commented that they did look a lot like Johnnie's elves.

Johnnie said," Ho, Ho, Ho" and Bill and Travis lifted their beer bottles in salute and clinked them together.

The next morning Alex went through her normal morning routine. She took her bike down the elevator and was surprised to see Johnnie waiting. He looked like he had not gotten any sleep, but his white teeth brightened an otherwise tired face.

The ride in was uneventful.

As usual, she and Johnnie were the first ones in. They both went to the locker room and changed into their working clothes. They stopped at the coffee area and got their coffee and went to their desks.

Johnnie took out a folder that contained three paper clipped stacks. He complimented Bill on organizing how the information was to be presented. He gave credit to Trey, the Chief, Bill, and Trevor for putting names into the columns.

He praised the Chief for identifying the person most likely at the top of the Bad Guy's List. It stood out prominently because it was the only name on the list.

He said that he had done a deep dive into that guy. And it was clear to him that he was a bad guy and that he had his dishonest money squirreled away in an offshore account.

Alex listened as Johnnie said that he would find that account. Once he found the account, he would contact her and get her permission to transfer the money to a bank account she would control.

He had also included a fourth category for the Mafia leader and the people that worked for him.

He figured the attack had been carried out by the mafia, so he had spent a great deal of time getting info about the leader and several of his leadership team.

He pointed out that there was a short "good guy's" list and a long "maybe bad guy's" list.

He let Alex know that by Monday she would have a much larger set of information, but she had enough ammo for the first round of the battle.

Alex took a quick look at the material and gave Johnnie a hug. She was just stepping back when she heard Trevor ask if he could get hug too.

Bill said that they had only brought in muffins but that the variety was great and if hugs were being given out, he would take one too.

Alex laughed and gave them each a hug and thanked them for helping Johnnie.

She then asked Johnnie if he wanted a muffin. Johnnie stood up and said he needed to refresh his coffee and would walk with her to the break area.

Alex was just putting her muffin on a napkin when Trey walked in. He had his luggage with him and said he would come back for his coffee and a muffin.

Alex returned to her desk but instead of sitting down she took the file that Johnnie had provided and went to the copy machine and made three copies.

She returned and gave Johnnie's copy back to him and thanked him for the miracle he had delivered.

She asked him how many hours of sleep that he had gotten.

She was not surprised when he replied with a question about what sleep meant.

She suggested he walk his bike home after eating his muffin and climb into bed.

Trevor again spoke up about his lack of sleep and could he go home as well?

Alex replied that he could do so if he had a report about the cops in Chicago to give her.

Bill chuckled and said that all Trevor could report on was the great time they had at Johnnie's apartment until Johnnie kicked them out.

The Chief came in and asked what Alex was doing in his office area and made the point that he had a new team coming in to take over her desk.

He held up his muffin and looked at Johnnie and said he looked like death warmed over and should go home as soon as possible.

He asked if he could have a copy of the report Johnnie had given to her.

Alex picked up the copy she had made and handed it to the Chief.

She said the only reason she was in was because Johnnie insisted that the Chief should get the first copy.

The Chief laughed and said that such actions went a long way in getting raises in his organization.

Alex followed the Chief into his office. She left the door open but asked the Chief to call the Illinois Lieutenant Governor and share the report with her. He should tell her that her new employee planned to confront the Chicago Police Department Deputy Chief that afternoon.

She asked him to communicate that she was not sure what the over the weekend action would be but that all requests put in by the Chicago Deputy Chief of Police should be denied or delayed.

The Chief asked Alex why she was asking him to make the call.

Alex replied that he was her boss and should remain in the loop. She planned to make sure the Lieutenant Governor understood that the assignment was a temporary one that would end when she, Alex decided that she had done all she could.

He nodded and thanked her for her attitude.

The call surprised the Lieutenant Governor. She said that she would make sure to keep the Deputy Chief of Police in check.

After the call, Alex said she was going to walk Johnnie back to his apartment and then go out to catch her flight.

During the walk back to the apartment she laughed when Johnnie said she owed him big time and that the price was a full tray of her cookies.

The flight to Chicago was just long enough for her to review Johnnie's report with Trey. She pointed out that Johnnie had identified the Mafia boss, his lieutenants, their holdings, their home addresses, the address of the mafia's current headquarters.

She said that she was amazed. She pointed out that Johnnie had included the names of the Mafia's boss biological family members and their addresses in Italy.

She then reviewed the information on the police force. He had only one name on bad guys list, but he had a detailed breakdown of that person.

He was Jesse Franklin the Assistant Chief of the Chicago Police department. He had his property in his wife's maiden name. He had unearthed the story about his wealth being passed on by his parents and the fact that Jesse had paid to bury his parents and the inheritance that was the cover for his wealth had never existed.

Alex told Trey that after they met with the Chicago Department Chief of Police, she planned to make a stop at Jesse Franklin's office and confront him as the caller that had threatened her.

She wanted to shake his world so he would make a mistake that she could use to arrest him.

Alex was met by a new driver at baggage claim recommended by her usual driver in Chicago who she had asked to meet Lindsey and Nolan. She asked him to take them to the main Chicago police station wait while she made a brief stop and afterwards take her home.

The drive to the police station was rather short.

As they arrived in front of the station Alex's personal internal alarm went off.

What she expected to see was a busy bustle of police going in and out of the station.

There were no police in sight.

She said one word to Trey, "trap."

She spotted the single black car parked across the street from the station.

She repeated "trap" and took her pistol out of her purse. She watched Trey take his out of his leg holster.

She told the driver to get under the dashboard when he stopped.

As Alex got out, two men got out of the black car. The one on her side was raising his shotgun when Alex shot him between the eyes and twice in the chest. His shotgun fired into the ground and the kick caused him to fall backwards.

Trey did the same with the other shooter. That shotgun went off and then went into the air like a rocket and fell back into the street.

Alex rushed the car and told the driver to keep his hands on the wheel, and he would live.

He immediately complied.

She took out his weapon and dropped it to the ground.

She looked around and there were still no police rushing in to help.

Finally, a police squad car arrived at the scene and reacted like she was the criminal and were ready to shoot her until Trey held up his badge and declared that he and his partner were Illinois Police Officers.

The front door of the station opened, and host of officers rushed out.

Alex knew it had been a hit set up by the Mafia and facilitated by the inside informant that sat at the top.

She planned to stop at his desk and confront him.

She gave the driver an additional tip and asked him to go someplace and wait for her call.

She walked into the station and was greeted by an old knurly sergeant sitting behind a well-worn desk that blocked the way.

He asked if she were responsible for the gun fire in front of the station.

When she said that yes she was, he said he was glad she had survived.

He then said that weapons would be checked unless she had official standing in the state of Illinois.

Alex looked at the sergeant and asked him if he recognized the name Jane Stradford her current boss.

He said he did indeed and waved her into the building.

Alex asked direction to the Chicago Police Chief's office. The Sergeant called to a young police officer and asked him to guide her to the Chief's office.

On the way she asked him to point out the office of the Assistant Chief.

Alex was greeted by the Chief's support, who made the point that she was five minutes late as she knocked on the Chief's office door.

She watched as the Chief put down the phone and came around the desk to shake hands.

He commented that he had just been on the phone with Jane and had gotten the quick update on events in Cincinnati.

He said he was pleased that she had survived an attempt on her life, and he hoped that she would do well in the assignment she had accepted.

Alex looked at Trey and said that she was looking forward to a very successful assignment and that she hoped for his support and the cooperation of his department.

The Chief responded that he and his leadership team would do all they could to make the assignment a success.

Alex made a mental note that this Chief was as political as they came and could not recognize corruption when it was under his nose, and he was out of touch with the people in his organization.

He was so disconnected that he was unaware of the incident that had just occurred in front of the Station.

Alex asked if he would have an office that she and Trey could use during her assignment and was told that his support would show her the one that was available just a few offices away.

His lack of questions about what she would be doing made it obvious that the Chief didn't have much interest in the assignment and was probably not expecting much from her and Trey.

She thanked him for his time and said that she had one more stop before departing for Evanston.

She said good day and got up and led the way out of the office.

It was only a short walk to the Department Deputy Chief's office.

She walked past an objecting support who was telling her she could not go in. She opened the office door and walked in.

She walked up to the Assistant Police Chief's desk, leaned in, and quietly called him Jesse, and reminded him that on his last call she had promised to find him and arrest him as a crooked cop.

She went on to tell him his threat had not worked.

The hit sent by his mafia friends to Cincinnati had not worked and the hit he had facilitated in front of the Chicago Police station had not worked.

She told him that he was on the hot plate and that he had the weekend to develop a list of all of his crooked associates as a way to getting her to recommend sending him to one of the white-collar prisons.

She said she would be back on Monday to take him into custody and put him behind bars and walked out.

Jessie sat looking at the door in a state of shock. He had never been outed in such a clear and precise fashion by anyone.

The Black detective from Cincinnati on special assignment as an Investigator for Lieutenant Governor, Jane Stradford had marched in and simply told him that his days of informing the Mafia and of covering for crooked cops was over.

How had she survived and how had she known he was the person who called her?

She had given him detailed banking information and purchases of his vacations, cars and other luxury items that far exceeded his salary by multiples.

He was in a full state of shock.

Alex had walked out of the Chicago Assistant Police Chief's office knowing that she had left him in a state of shock.

As she and Trey got to the curb a black car squealed to a stop in front of them and two gunmen holding silencer equipped handguns jumped out and said that they were extending an invitation to meet with their boss.

Alex decided against making any move against the two. She said she would come along without creating a scene.

She relinquished her purse but when they pulled out the hoods to put over her and Trey's heads, she said that if they were taking them to the boss's headquarters on the fifth floor of the Long-Distance trucking company at 634 North Lakeshore Drive, they did not need the hoods.

She pointed out that she already knew the way.

The thug that had exited from the back of the car simply said "damn" and got in and sat in the middle.

The gunman that had the front seat waved his gun and told Trey to get in behind the driver.

He waved the gun at Alex pointing to the seat behind him and closed the door.

He got into the front and told the driver to go to the office.

Alex sat watching the flashes of the view of the lake and thanked Johnnie for having given her the information he had dug up.

She owned him big time and would let him know that she had two trays of cookies coming his way.

Alex took note of how long the elevator took to get from the basement garage to the fifth floor. She also noted that the boss's office was at the other end of the hall from the elevators.

She was sure that none of her observations mattered what mattered was what would transpire in the office.

The mafia boss leaned back in his high-backed plush desk chair.

He smiled and said, "Well, I finally get to meet the great "Cincinnati Black Annie Oakley."

Alex smiled and replied, "And I get to meet the great Gennaro Visentino, if I get lucky, I will get to meet his wife the famous and beautiful Italian Actress. If I am even luckier you will invite me to come your house and enjoy dinner out by your pool."

The room went silent.

Alex knew she had struck a nerve.

Gennaro quietly responded that he knew where her lover lived, where her parents lived and worked. He reminded her that he had warned her against taking the assignment and that taking it would result in grave consequences.

Alex again leaned in and gave the names of his parents, his brother, his two sisters and their addresses in Italy. She said if one of her family were to be hurt in any way, she had the connections to make sure he paid in full.

Gennaro looked at the piece of paper that was turned face down on his desk. It was a warning to keep his hands off of Alex Evercrest or face a grave consequence.

It was from the Gulf Cartel.

He had never received such a message and had discounted it.

Who was this person and how had she gotten hold of all the information he had tried to protect?

He was the power in Chicago. He wondered if this detective knew of the warning to him from the Gulf Cartel.

If she did, it would not do her any good.

She would not make it out of Chicago on this fateful day.

She was soon going to be face down in the river.

Alex watched as Gennaro thought through her response.

She was not surprised by his reply of touche and did not for a moment think that he planned to let her live through the rest of the day.

He said that if she went easy on the number of bad police officers that she identified, he would look the other way.

Alex responded that she would keep that in mind.

Gennaro leaned back in his chair and thanked Alex for coming to see him.

Alex stood and said that she would get her driver to pick her up at the curb.

Gennaro shock his head and insisted that his driver would take them back to the station.

Alex looked at Trey and said, "see I told you he only wanted to meet with me," and stood up.

The two gunmen had been silent with their guns held in front of them. The gunman who sat in front turned and opened the door. The gunman who sat in the middle in the back seat waved his gun for them to follow.

She heard Gennaro instruct them to give the two a smooth ride. She hesitated a moment at the entrance to the elevator and let Trey bump into her. She turned and apologized for being so slow. Trey replied that it was his fault. The gunman in back gave them both a push.

She and Trey had just agreed who each of them would kill.

The ride back seemed to be going smoothly. The sun was painting a beautiful red, yellow and pink tapestry on the puffy white clouds out over the lake.

Alex made a comment about its beauty.

The driver said he agreed.

He was told to be quiet and get them to their destination.

A few moments later Alex knew that they were not going back to the station and that they were going to go to some dark location along the Chicago River.

She asked if they were taking a tour of Chicago and was told to shut up.

Alex knew for sure that they were being taken to a killing zone.

She had her hands on her lap and noted that Trey had his hands on his lap. She hoped the gunmen planned to get them out of the car before shooting them.

The car turned up a dark alley and came to a stop at the edge of a dock that extended into the Chicago River.

Alex saw the dark ribbon of water and knew they had arrived at the execution site.

She faked a sneeze and immediately drove her belt knife into the temple of the gunman in the front seat. She effortlessly took the gun from the dead gunman and immediately told the drive to put his hands on the wheel or die.

She looked over at Trey who had the other gunman's weapon in his hand.

Trey reached over the driver's left shoulder and took out the driver's gun.

Alex got out and went to the driver's window and had him lower it.

Trey then got out.

Alex told the driver to remind his boss that she knew his home address where he and his model wife lived, and she would soon be out to get him.

She made a call to the phone number that Johnnie had provided.

When Gennaro answered Alex told him that he and his team were now in her sights.

She hung up.

She then told Trey to call Lindsey and the Sheriff in Loveland while she called Matt and the Chief.

She asked the Chief to contact Johnnie, Bill, and Travis.

She then called her mother to warn her to be on guard.

Finally, she called the driver that she had tipped and asked him to pick her up. She told him that she was somewhere along the Chicago River and gave him her phone number so he could find her via her phone.

Trey reminded Alex that Lindsey was in transit to Chicago on her way to Alex's parent's house.

Alex called the driver she normally used and found out that he was standing holding the hand of young Nolan as they waited for the luggage.

Her replacement driver flashed his front lights as he slowed to a stop to pick her up.

After they had gone a few blocks, Alex said that she would pay extra for a fast ride to her destination. She was surprised at the increase in speed.

They arrived at the loop in front of her parent's house in record time.

Her mother, father and Matt came out to greet her. She saw Harold Zimmerman standing outside of the front door.

She gave her parents hugs and then took Matt into her arms and gave him a long kiss. Then she asked where he had been when she called him to make sure he had protection.

Matt gave a short chuckle and thanked her for giving him a first class ticked to use. When he got her call, he told his team he was on his way to Chicago and went to the airport. He had taken her advice to always look like a professional traveler. Thanks to having a first-class ticket was able to get on a flight. He said he figured that being in transit would be the best way to be safe.

Alex smiled and agreed that he had chosen the best way to protect himself and gave him another kiss.

She would learn the next day that her friends knew how to make sure she would be protected from the Mafia and corrupt police officers.

There would be no doubt that those that threatened her wellbeing would pay a dear price.

15 Ultimatum

Gennaro read through the warning from the Gulf Cartel for the third time.

He was amazed that the cartel would put out a protection order for a lowly Black detective from the little city of Cincinnati.

Of what importance was she to the Cartel and who did the cartel think they were dealing with?

He was the power in Chicago.

He had the larger organization.

What were they up to in protecting a law enforcement officer?

Who was this Alex Evercrest?

How did the cartel even know about her and that she was coming to Chicago?

What really got his goat was that they had also threatened him with serious retribution.

Damn he thought to himself, he was the power in Chicago.

He had the people.

They were seconds not firsts.

His organization was first.

He ran Chicago.

He did what he wanted in Chicago and well beyond.

Retribution, really!

Who did they think they were dealing with?

What impressed him about his target was that she had survived two of his ordered assassination attempts. He was impressed with the manner that she had killed four of his top assassins as if they were amateurs.

It was clear to him that she made her gun talk when she pulled it from her holster. She was a rare individual that acted with a deadly skill and a focused purpose.

He was down four gunmen who had for years successfully carried out their kill assignments.

He was looking forward to personally confronting this, Alex Evercrest. Afterwards he planned to have her swimming face down in the Chicago River.

The cartel would see how he dealt with threats of retribution.

He was the power in Chicago and no two-bit detective from a hick town like Cincinnati was going to change that.

He sent his personal bodyguards to pick her up and bring her to him. They had called ahead and let him know that she knew where the offices were located.

That surprised him!

He watched as two people were brought into his office.

Her smile and greeting of, "I hope all is well with you," caught him by surprise.

He had expected her to be angry and somewhat overcome.

Instead, she acted like they were good friends, and she had come in for a friendly chat.

Her partner was at least a foot taller than her diminutive stature. He looked much more of a threat then she did.

He wondered how tough he might be.

He was surprised that they had been made special investigators of the Illinois Lieutenant Governor's office.

That was a unique angle, but it would afford her no protection.

He had no desire to tangle with that branch, but he also had no fear of his capability to neutralize the Lieutenant Governor.

He looked down at his desk to make sure that the warning message was turned over.

His glance down made him think about a poker game. A game that he knew he had the best hand.

He then looked at her and made the point that he had sent her a warning not to take the assignment. He reminded her that she had pushed her friends and loved ones in front of a bus.

He did not expect the reply she gave him.

She stepped up to his desk, leaned in at him and let him know that she knew where he and his model wife lived, where his family lived in Italy and then from memory named each of them.

He was stunned and wondered how she had been able to get information that he had been sure was not accessible in any specific location. She had named every close relative that he had.

He asked himself how she could possibly have gotten that information.

He was taken aback when she apologized about threatening innocent people in his family. She then said she was withdrawing her threat on his biological family and was instead letting him know that she would instead avenge any harm to her family by eliminating his Mafia family in Chicago and in Italy.

She then named each of his current lieutenants. He was shocked.

He immediately concluded that she had to die.

She knew too much.

She had to die.

He wanted to laugh and tell her that she had sealed her fate and had volunteered for the bullet that would kill her.

He wanted to shoot her immediately, but he held his anger.

He often attended terminations along the river and wished he could do so this time, but he needed to keep as far away from this kill as possible.

He was sure that there would be a large scale follow up investigation trying to pin the murder on his organization.

He would need to be satisfied with celebrating her floating face down in the river.

He thanked her for coming to see him and told his personal enforcers to take her back to the station.

They already knew what was to happen next.

Once they had left, he called a meeting of his leadership team for a celebration to take place in the leadership room. He ordered in refreshments and a bottle of his best Courvoisier. He had been saving the bottle for an appropriate significant event. He now had such an event.

He had no idea that the Cartel had a mole in his organization and that his ignoring of their warning had already put in motion their response.

The cartel was on the way.

Gennaro took a long drag on his Cuban cigar.

His team arrived and he explained that they would be celebrating the demise of the upstart detective that had killed four of their own and who had ignored his warning against going to work for the Illinois Lieutenant Governor.

He let them know that he was expecting a call from his personal bodyguards that she was face down in the Chicago River.

They all gave a cheer.

He personally poured each of his lieutenants a shot and passed them out.

He looked at the wall clock. The call he was eagerly waiting for seemed to be taking longer than he was expecting.

When his phone rang and the voice on the other end simply said, "My body count is up to six and now you are in my cross hairs. You and your leadership team need to hunker down." I am on my way to put you in your place."

"Stay away from my family."

"Guard your Mafia family. I will come to get them all."

Then the line went dead.

He did not know what to do. The entire room had gone silent as they listened to the phone that he had put in the speaker mode.

He picked up his shot of Courvoisier and downed it. He savored the hot streak going down his throat.

His leadership team were all looking at him and wondering what to do.

He was about to explain when the meeting room door seemed to explode and shatter inward.

Six hooded gunmen entered. They shot each of the people in the room.

Gennaro was last to be killed. He died with thinking of the warning he had ignored.

He was not going to be around make them pay.

How they had learned about his action was a mystery that he would never learn.

He died with the realization that the "Cincinnati Black Annie Oakley" had the ultimate protection of the Gulf Cartel.

His last thought was "damn".

One of the Gunmen put a business card on the table under Gennaro's hand, and all the gunmen left.

A few moments later his personal driver, who had been sent back with a message from Alex, entered the conference room. He stopped when he saw all the bodies.

He turned, went to where his personal car was parked and left the building.

The retribution that Gennaro had threatened Alex with had been negated and he had paid the ultimate price for ignoring the warning to stay away from her.

15 Ultimatum

16 The Yin and the Yang

*T*he Chief left the office and drove slowly home. He decided he needed to sit out on his deck and somehow decompress.

The recent events that were, on the one hand a great opportunity and on the other hand put one of his best investigative teams into the line of fire, represented competing yin-yang of his emotions.

He needed to decompress. He would feel much better when Alex was back working in from her desk in Cincinnati.

Mary-Ann brought out a cheese plate with crackers and some fresh fruit and sat down and asked what was bothering him.

He confided in her that he felt that he had traded Alex's safety for his desire to set up two additional detective teams. He explained the arrangement that he had signed off on with the Illinois Lieutenant Governor to have Alex identify the crooked cops in the Chicago police department.

He admitted that the generous monetary offer was very attractive and that he had already received praise from all the Cincinnati area leadership for arranging such a great the deal.

Mary-Ann asked if he had directed Alex to take the assignment.

He responded that Alex had made the offer even more attractive by insisting that both her salary and Trey's salary be guaranteed for one year even if their assignment was completed early.

The salary she negotiated was thirty percent higher than their current salary and she had suggested he apply the remainder of their current Cincinnati salary toward setting up the additional detective teams.

Mary-Anne smiled and pointed out that it seemed that Alex was the one that was in control of the negotiations and that he was simply the beneficiary of her keen negotiation skills.

She reminded him that Alex had repeatedly surprised them and that she had made their lives much more exciting.

She said that she always looked forward to Alex's next assignment and the whirlwind action that accompanied it.

She handed him another piece of cheese and told him that she was going in to prepare dinner and he should have another sip of wine and relax.

He should just make sure that Alex had everything that his group could provide.

He felt better but he was still worried about Alex's safety.

He was still sitting out on the deck when he received the call from Alex about the threat from the Chicago Mafia boss to kill her friends and loved ones.

She let him know about the ambush in front of the Chicago police station and the fact that no police were present when two shooters stepped out of a black limo guns drawn ready to shoot.

She let him know that she and Trey had shot and killed them before the two could fire their slug loaded shotguns.

She then shared the fact that after her introductory meeting with the Chicago Chief of Police and the Assistant Chief of police, she and Trey had been kidnapped at the curb side outside the of the police station. They were taken to meet with the Chicago Mafia boss.

The boss threatened to kill her family and friends.

She said that thanks to Johnnie's thorough research she was able to threaten him with her own retribution if he took any vindictive action.

He had indicated that she had made her point, and he would have her taken back to the police station.

She had left the meeting with assurances that she would be taken back to the police station, but she and Trey were driven to the Chicago River to be disposed of.

The two taking them were dead and she had sent the driver back with a message to the boss that he was now in her gun sights.

She was calling him to alert him to the threat from the mafia leader and asked him to call Johnnie, Bill and Trevor and warn them.

She said she would take care of contacting Matt and her parents, and Trey was contacting Lindsey.

She apologized for putting he and Mary-Anne in danger.

As the call was coming to an end, he thanked her and told her to take extra care of herself.

After hanging up he went in and retrieved his weapon and made sure the doors were locked. He made the calls to Johnnie, Bill, and Trevor.

He then went into the kitchen and let Mary-Ann know about the situation.

She shook her head and said that she was not surprised at the speed at which events were occurring. She asked if her body count of six bad guys was accurate.

He assured her that it was at least that high.

He experienced a restless night and was up several times.

He still had a nagging feeling that he was not doing enough to protect Alex.

He was having breakfast and had turned on the news channel to get the latest news.

Usually, the headline of Breaking News just meant that the channel wanted viewers not to change channels. This time he almost fell out of his chair.

The breaking news was that the police had been called to a location on the north side of Chicago where the body of the Chicago mafia leader and six other men had been found in a meeting room and two additional bodies were found in a limo in the parking garage.

The Chicago Police Chief gave a report of the investigation and said that the Mafia boss was holding a card stating that threats to Black Angels would be avenged.

He came to the realization that he was the supervisor of a detective that was protected by a drug cartel.

It was unheard of!

He thought about it and smiled as he thought about Alex's ability of lining up ardent supporters and in the case of lining up a cartel she had scored big.

Their protection had the ultimate sting of death.

The Chief made calls to Johnnie, Bill and Trevor and suggested they tune into the latest news coming out of Chicago.

He thanked them for activating their friends south of the border.

He was sure that the action taken had been done by the Gulf Cartel.

They were the only ones that would dare to take such a dramatic action against the Mafia.

He hoped that the Cartel and the Mafia did not engage in a full out battle but at the moment he was overjoyed that the action taken had removed the immediate threat to Alex and Trey.

He was counting on the cartel to handle the Mafia's response in a manner that left Alex in the clear.

Now all he had to worry about were the bad cops in the Chicago police department.

He made a call to Alex and asked if she was aware about the breaking news out of Chicago.

She said she was out fishing with her family and Trey's family but would turn on the news.

After wishing Alex a good weekend, he set up a conference call with Johnnie, Bill, and Trevor.

He shared the events that Alex had shared with him and then he asked who had figured out how to get cartel protection for Alex.

Johnnie's laugh and a halfhearted denial and Bill's "no clue" comment was all he needed to know that the three he was talking to had somehow arranged the cartel protection.

He had told them to have Alex's back but now he knew that at the time he had no idea what that would mean.

He figured it was probably a good idea to drop the question.

He commented that he a had gotten notification of their raises.

He asked if the three were available for a brat and beer at his house that afternoon.

He wanted to get their take on the events that had transpired.

17 Arrival

Rose-Ann thought getting Alex to root out corruption in the Chicago legal system was one of her brighter ideas. Having followed all of Alex's cases, she knew that though corruption in the Chicago legal system was deeply rooted she was sure Alex would successfully charge through it and clear it up.

She had been so focused on Alex's ability to bring in the "bad guys" that she overlooked the fact that the risk would be overwhelming.

She was looking forward to Alex spending time at home and using their library office. She was surprised that Russel did not seem to have the same enthusiasm for having his daughter coming to work in Chicago.

He stated that he thought it was too dangerous.

He made the point that in Cincinnati, Alex had the police department as support

In Chicago she would have the police department as an adversary and at the best the organization would be hands off.

He made the point that though the Police Department represented a huge threat, the Mafia represented an even bigger threat.

Rose-Anne had reached out to her long-time friend from her college years who was now the Illinois Lieutenant Governor and suggested that she look into hiring Alex to solve the Chicago police corruption issue. She was surprised at how enthusiastic Jane had been about the idea of getting Alex assigned to such a task.

Not long after, Jane shared the fact that she had sent a proposal to the Cincinnati Chief of detectives asking for Alex's services. She said the proposal included a significant monetary incentive for such a service and that she was waiting for a reply.

Shortly after getting Jane's message, Alex called and asked her about the offer and that she remembered Jane as one of her friends. Alex wanted to know if she had been the catalyst that triggered the offer.

Rose-Ann admitted that the frustration created by dealing with corrupt cops when they were called to testify in court and lied had triggered her to call her longtime friend and make the suggestion.

Alex sympathized with the situation but let her know that frustration on her part was not enough for her daughter to agree to the deal.

A few days later, she was surprised when Jane called her and let her know that Alex had negotiated a deal that financially stretched her departments budget.

Jane had given a little laugh and shared the fact that she had accused Alex of being a tougher negotiator than her mother.

The deal Alex negotiated was almost twice the size than the one she had initially proposed. She also shared that Alex had insisted that she and her partner would be sworn in as Illinois special investigators, on special assignment, reporting only to the Lieutenant Governor's office. She had insisted that her position should out rank the Chicago Chief of Police.

Jane said the swearing in ceremony had occurred immediately after she agreed to Alex's demands and that Alex, and her partner were now official Illinois detectives working for her on special assignment.

Rose-Anne thanked Jane for having gone through with the offer and agreeing to Alex's terms.

On Tuesday, Alex called and let her know about the contract with Jane and that she intended to be at the house on Friday afternoon. Alex said that she and Trey planned to stay at the house and that Lindsey and Nolan would also be coming up on weekends while the Chicago assignment lasted.

Alex had let her know the Friday flight she planned to be on.

It was hard for Rose-Ann to control her enthusiasm.

She loved the idea of Alex working from the house. More than a year ago, she had enjoyed having Lindsey and Nolan at the house when Russel had invited what turned out to be the whole Cincinnati detective unit to go fishing.

She closed by promising a home cooked dinner on Friday evening.

The Thursday morning news out of Cincinnati highlighted the shooting that took place when two men, apparently hit men, had been killed.

Rose Ann immediately scanned every channel for more information. She was sure the attack had been on Alex.

Russel's comment about the danger involved with such an assignment hit her like a slap on the face.

She flipped. She immediately called Alex to tell her not to take the assignment.

Alex replied that it was too late and that pandora's box had been opened and there was no way to close it.

She was still coming up on Friday and after a brief stop at the Police Station, she and Trey would be coming home. She said that Lindsey and Nolan would be arriving Friday afternoon as well.

Rose Ann thought about the old adage about being careful what one wished for.

She now worried about Alex's safety.

It was worse than being frustrated by crooked cops.

She realized that she had let her frustration blind her and that she had taken a selfish action.

Now she worried about her only child.

She turned her focus on getting ready for the weekend.

She decided to work from home on Friday so she could prepare some of the food that needed to be in the oven.

Alex's next call to tell her that Harold Zimmerman from the DEA would be arriving at the house to protect her from a potential mob attempt on her life frightened her.

Alex let her know that she had also called her father and had told him to put a chair against the doorknob and to contact a security guard he trusted to come and protect him.

Rose-Anne could not believe that such action was necessary. When Alex shared that she had just shot and killed two would be assassins on her arrival to Chicago, she realized that her request for help with corrupt police and judges was more dangerous than she had ever anticipated.

Alex let her know that she was going into the station and would let her know when she was on her way home. She suggested that Harold and anyone with him be invited to dinner.

Soon after, Harold and three others arrived. After a brief greeting, he positioned the three with him at key locations in the house.

The opening of the garage door got an immediate swat team like response. Russel got out of his car and put his hands up. She rushed to him and gave him a hug.

She began to explain but he said he knew about the risk. He said he had come home early because he felt that it would be safer at home than trying to hunker down in his office. He greeted Harold and thanked him for coming to the house.

He hoped the guarding was being done unofficially so they could enjoy a beer together.

They all went into the house and Rose Ann let them know that she was expecting a call from Alex to let her know that she was on the way.

More than an hour passed and there was no call. She began to worry and thought about calling Alex, but Harold cautioned against it.

He said he too was worried but a call at the wrong time might put Alex in danger.

That only caused her to worry more.

The doorbell rang and the DEA agents all reacted.

Harold had his gun drawn as he opened the door.

Matt dropped his bag and put his hands in the air and said, "I give"

Rose-Anne rushed forward and gave him a hug and pulled him in so the door could be closed. She said that she did not know that he was coming.

He let her know that he received Alex's cryptic call to get security protection. He decided that being in transit was safer than any other way to be safe, so he had taken a flight to Chicago.

He knew that Alex would not have sent out such a message if she was in control.

He planned to be where he might be able to help.

He looked around and said that he had expected to be greeted by a surprised Alex and wondered where she was.

Rose-Anne was now in tears.

She went into the kitchen to try and get over her anxiety.

She felt like it was her fault and said a little prayer.

The ride to Alex's parent's home gave Trey a few moments to decompress from the events of the day.

He looked at Alex, shook his head, and thanked her for once again getting them out of a jam.

She smiled and pointed out that he had done his job with the thug sitting between them. That thug was going to shoot her. She pointed out that they had survived as a they always did, as a team.

She sent out several key messages.

One was an arrest warrant request for Jesse Franklin. She got confirmation that she would have that by Saturday afternoon.

She then sent a note to Johnnie asking him to give her what he had on the list of crooked cops.

She sent one to the Chief and to Jane Stafford, Illinois Lieutenant Governor, to update them on her plans for the coming week.

She finally felt ready for Monday morning. She shared her thoughts with Trey who nodded and voiced his agreement.

She then suggested that they think about enjoying the weekend.

They would have their hands full in the following week. They would have to be careful not to be shot by a crooked cop or more mafia hit men.

She suggested that they focus on enjoying Nolan, playing Chutes and Ladders, and fishing.

Trey laughed and said he would enjoy fishing if they got to do it without being shot at.

His phone rang. It was Lindsey checking in and letting him know that she and Nolan were just leaving the airport and heading for Alex's parents, and they would be there in about forty-five minutes to an hour.

Alex called her mother. She found out that her father was home, and they were wondering what had taken her so long.

Alex deflected giving an explanation and then reminded her mother that Lyndsey and Nolan were on the way from the airport.

She then sat back and asked her driver how his family was doing and what they planned for the holidays.

That got him talking and she sat back and relaxed.

She would later be amazed by the action that the "Angel on the Hill" and put into motion on behalf of the "Black Angel of the North."

18 Weekend

Alex perked up as the car turned into the lane. She loved the approach to the house. Over the years the trees had grown and now made a canopy across the lane. She remembered helping plant them. She took out a twenty and as she got out and thanked the driver for making good time. The twenty was in addition to the tip she had already done online and the one she had given after the shooting in front of the Chicago police station. He thanked her, gave his card, and told her to call him any time day or night.

She knew that she now had two drivers that would respond to her call.

She and Trey had traveled light and had asked Lindsey to bring up their two large suitcases.

Alex tried the door, but it was locked. She rang the doorbell and was met with the business end of a gun barrel in Harold Z's hand.

She raised her hands and said, "I give."

Harold gave a small laugh and said that she was the second person to use the same line.

Rose-Ann pulled Alex in as she gave her a hug.

As her mother was about to speak Alex put her finger to her mother's lips and told her not to say she was sorry.

Alex stopped as Matt came around the corner. She asked what he was doing in her house and laughed as he said that he had done what she had told him to do.

He said that she had told him to get to a safe place and what safer place could he find than her house that was protected by the DEA and her mother.

Alex pulled him to her and gave him a languishing kiss. She said that she was glad that he had followed her instructions so well.

Her mother again began to apologize for getting Alex into a dangerous situation.

Alex turned to her and asked if she had negotiated the contract with Jane. Then she asked if she had arranged for her to be an employee in Jane's office.

Her mother started to say, "no but... and Alex said that she should stop because, she, Alex, had done the negotiation and she and Trey were the ones sworn in.

She went on to say that it was her fault that the DEA had to be at their home to protect the family.

It had been her audacity to challenge the Mafia leader and to counter his threats that had led to the current situation they were in.

She was the one that should be apologizing.

Trey let Harold know that he expected Lindsey and Nolan at any moment, and he wanted to greet them without a gun.

Harold said he would stand back and only shoot if Trey went down in a hail of bullets.

Alex took Matt's hand and went to the kitchen. Her father followed them and offered to make her some tea.

Her mother was close behind but when the doorbell rang. she turned back to the foyer.

Trey knew that Lindsey and Nolan had arrived and were unaware of the events of the afternoon. Trey gave them both hugs and suggested they go sit out by the pool and enjoy all the snacks that Rose-Anne had prepared.

As they made their way through the kitchen, he looked at Alex and said that he was going to enjoy the weekend in the safest home in the US and after waiting for a session of hugs and kissed led the way to the poolside area.

Alex took her tea and went out and took a seat by the pool

She listened as her mother informed everyone what was for dinner.

Harold Z let her mother know that he and his team would take a raincheck because they had all left their offices in a hurry and were expected home for dinner. He pointed to Alex and Trey and said that the family protectors had arrived and those that cared enter had better not be packing.

Alex shook her head, smiled, and thanked him for having done her a favor and if he or any team member wanted to do some fishing on Sunday, they should let her know.

It would be her treat.

Nolan asked her if he could go swimming. Alex knew it was a cool evening, but the pool was heated. She pointed to Trey and Lindsey and said that they were the ones to decide.

Lindsey looked at Trey and asked him to carry the suitcases up and she would take Nolan up to get ready.

Alex said that she was going to take a quick shower before dinner.

She had rolled her suitcase to the foot of the stairs when Matt took hold of the handle and said that for the price of a shower, he would carry the suitcase to her room.

Alex laughed and accused him of taking advantage of her.

He responded that he would do so as often as possible.

Rose-Anne looked at Russel and said that she still felt guilty about the danger she had lured her daughter into.

Russel agreed that she was a catalyst, but that Alex was the one that had decided, and he agreed with Alex that the subject of blame should be dropped.

Nolan, and Lindsey were the first to return. And Nolan immediately jumped into the pool.

The sound of Nolan laughing as he repeatedly jumped in and then got out lightened the atmosphere.

When Trey returned Rose-Anne asked what had taken, he and Alex, so long in Chicago.

Trey replied that he would wait until Alex was present before saying anything.

Russel handed him a specialty beer as a way to divert the subject. He figured that they would hear what the news casters would report in the morning.

Alex and Matt came out of the family room to the pool area. They were wearing matching sweat suits.

Lindsey commented that they looked like fashion models.

Alex thanked her and commented that she wanted to see if she could become a fat lady. She said she and Trey had skipped lunch knowing they would have a feast when they got to her house.

Rose-Anne said that she would throw in a favorite desert for a recounting of what had taken them so long to arrive.

Alex looked at Nolan and asked her mother to wait until after dinner.

Nolan looked at Alex and said that he knew that she was going to share some tale about people trying to kill her and that she had killed them. He said he knew that she had saved him in his house and that she had later saved his dad.

Alex laughed and gave him a hug. She said he had it about right but she wanted to tell it so it could scare the old people. and she did not want to scare him.

Nolan nodded his head and said that he wanted to sleep tight that night so he would turn in after desert if his dad read him a bedtime story.

Alex always looked forward to her mother's cooking. Her mother was a certified chef and often pulled in other chefs to help her with large parties.

Alex enjoyed the pasta primavera consisting of a variety of mixed vegetables and a generous number of shrimp. The seasoning was unique and delivered a taste that she had never experienced before but really enjoyed.

Rose-Anne announced that dessert was a choice of Crème Brulé or Apple Pie with vanilla ice cream or both.

Nolan and Trey chose the apple pie. Alex asked Matt if he would split with her. She would take the Crème Brulé if he took the apple pie.

After desert Trey took Nolan up to the bedroom to read him a bedtime story.

When he returned Alex said she would share what had happened to her and Trey from the beginning.

She began by describing the offer from the Illinois Lieutenant Governor and said that she initially was planning to turn it down.

She took time to ask for her team's opinion about the offer. They agreed with her that it was an impossible job. Their opinion put weight on the side of her rejecting the offer.

She and Matt were walking back to the office when an anonymous threatening call made her change her mind.

The call crystallized her decision to accept. Once she decided to take the assignment, she thought through what it would take to succeed. She knew she would want to be an Illinois official that had more power than the Chicago Police Chief.

She figured she and Trey should receive combat pay so she got them a thirty percent pay raise.

She needed the power to arrest and jail so she could immediately lock up any individual that she found to be corrupt.

And she knew she would need multiple miracles to identify the bad cops.

So, she negotiated to have Johnnie be her data analyst and personal miracle maker be her Cincinnati backup. She got him the highest raise possible.

The requirements she stipulated were met by Jane Stratford and by her own Chief.

She and Trey were sworn in immediately after the acceptance of her terms.

The Chief had agreed to have Johnnie work on delivering the miracles she needed.

Alex then shared the arrival on the following morning of two hit men that came to her apartment. She looked around the pool side and quietly said that she shot and killed both. She made the point that she had not tried to arrest them, and she did not give them a fighting chance.

Trey commented that the hit men had fire a slug twelve gauge shotgun and were not there to give her a chance, and she did exactly what she should have done.

He then took up the narrative and said that they flew to Chicago and took a car to the police Station to introduce themselves to the Chief of Police and to see about an office where they would work.

They arrived at the police station and not one policeman was in sight.

A single black limo was parked across the street from the main entrance to the police station.

Alex had quietly told him "ambush." Alex got out and killed one shooter and he killed the other.

Then Alex got the driver of the limo to tell her who had set up the hit. He did not mention that she hit him on the side of the head when he hesitated to tell her and that she put the gun to his head.

All he shared was that she got the information she asked for.

"We went in and introduced ourselves to the Chief of Police," Alex continued.

"Then thanks to Johnnie's sleuthing I was able to go into the Assistant Chief's office and confront him as the police connection to the Chicago Mafia."

"As we left the building, we were kidnapped from in front of the police station and taken to meet with Gennaro Visentino," Trey continued.

Johnnie delivered the miracle information that saved their lives that afternoon. They both owed him big time.

Alex shared that she was able to keep from being hooded by letting the head gunman know she knew the address where they were going and with whom they would meet.

"Again, thanks to Johnnie, I was able to counter Gennaro's threats against our family with threats against he and his family.

Johnnie had given her Gennaro's entire family tree with names and addresses.

But I clarified that unlike his threat I would eliminate his Mafia family not his biological one.

Gennaro verbally indicated that he accepted a tie and would let them go back to the station. But instead, they were taken to a spot along the Chicago River to be killed."

"I learned from Alex's experience and now have a belt buckle like hers that has a small knife. And we each killed the two assassins as soon as the car came to a stop. Alex sent the driver back to Gennaro with the message that he had broken his word and now he and his mafia family were the target." Trey shared.

"I placed the call to each of you immediately afterwards and arranged for protection with Harold Z and warned everyone else to take protective action. And now you know what has transpired." Alex concluded.

Rose-Anne asked what she planned to do on Monday morning and how should they think about the threat from the Mafia.

Alex looked around and said that they would need continued protection. She planned to call her old boss the sheriff in Zion to see if he could provide protection for the family.

She and Trey would need to recruit a few honest cops to provide them some protection when they were in Chicago.

She then said that she was planning on getting some sleep so that she could wake up early and go fishing.

As her eyes closed for the night, she had no idea about the sea of death that had already taken place.

She went to sleep with thoughts of watching Nolan fishing and her father cooking the brats she loved to eat.

19 The Catch

*T*he next morning getting ready to go fishing seemed a little surreal and took Alex back through memory lane. She and her father had often gotten up in the wee hours to go fishing.

Fishing with him and later eating the fish prepared by her mother were sweet memories that she cherished. This morning, she brought herself forward to the current moment as she felt Matt's warmth. She placed her hand on his bare chest and relaxed as she woke up.

She pushed herself to get up and get moving. She could smell the coffee her mother had brewing in the kitchen. She got up and got dressed. She woke Matt up and told him he would find her in the Kitchen.

Once everyone was up and ready, they all got into her father's conversion van and drove to the harbor.

The sky was pitch black and the stars still bright as Alex led the way into the bait shop.

Felix, the owner of the marina, came around the counter and gave her a hug. He said he insisted that they take his yacht out to go fishing.

He said he had it all prepared and ready to go and that he would not take no for an answer. He chuckled and said that he had taken her father's boat out of the water to make sure she accepted. He was sure he still owed her big time for the time his college friend had shot up the yacht and had tried to kill her.

She thanked him for the use of the yacht, but she insisted on donating to his favorite charity.

She thanked him for having put the breakfast and lunch meals and snacks on board.

Felix said that the bait and gear had already been loaded as well. Alex thanked him and then took Nolan's hand and asked if he was ready to go fishing.

She smiled when he nodded and pulled on her hand. Her father, Matt and her mother led the way toward the yacht. She and Nolan were next, and Lindsey and Trey brought up the rear.

She knew that she was building another memory that she would treasure for years.

The sky was still black, and the stars painted a swath of twinkling bright lights across the heavens as she and Trey cast off the lines and then jumped on board as Matt under the direction of her father backed the yacht away from the pier and pointed it out to the exit of the bay.

Alex sat down at one of the side benches and pulled out a muffin. It and a cup of coffee brought the morning into focus. After a few moments she prepared her fishing pole and set it aside.

She watched as Trey prepared three poles.

She then made sure her father's and Matt's poles were ready as well.

Then she turned to her mother and asked her about the cases she was handling.

Her mother shook her head and said that she preferred to talk about how they should prepare the fish and what the afternoon and evenings activities should be for Nolan.

The sun began painting the scattered fluffy clouds pink and yellow with a hint of purple. Alex pointed one cloud out to Nolan and asked what animal it made him think of.

Nolan immediately said it was Dumbo. He then got into looking for other shapes and the cloud spotting game continued until they reached the fishing spot.

The fishing spots on the boat got chosen, the fishing lines were cast, and everyone was eager for their first bite.

Alex had just landed a nice sized bass when her phone rang. She was surprised that it was working so far from shore until she remembered that the yacht had a radio connection with the harbor bait shop.

It was the Chief calling.

He asked if she had seen the breaking morning news out of Chicago.

She let him know that she was fishing with Nolan and the rest of the family.

She knew that it was important when the Chief insisted that she take the time to see the news. He reminded her that the yacht had a tv that was able to get the news channels.

Alex said she would turn it on and tune in the news. She thanked him for the call.

She turned on the screen and selected one of the news channels. The red banner declaring breaking news was painted across the bottom of the screen.

She was surprised to see that the announcer was standing in front of the building where she and Trey had been taken. He reported that seven people had been shot and killed in a meeting room on the fifth floor and two more bodies were found in a limo in the basement parking lot. The police had learned of the shooting when an anonymous 911 call had been received.

Alex looked at Trey who had joined her along with everyone but Matt who was still at the helm of the yacht.

The news caster speculated that it was a hit by the Mafia.

Alex looked at Trey and commented that the announcer was close, but it was Gennaro and his leadership team who had been killed and the two bodies in the car had been the ones they had sent back.

All the dead were the Mafia!

She was about to wonder about who might have done the shooting when the announcer made a comment about a mysterious card that mentioned something about angels had been in the hand of one of the victims.

Alex knew immediately who was responsible.

She sent a text to the "Angel on the Hill" and her brother Adolfo.

It simply said "Thank You"

She had no clue how Angelica, the angel on the hill and the wife of the former Gulf Cartel leader had somehow learned of the situation.

Alex could only think of one person who would have known to ask for help.

A short time later, after they had all had time to discuss the dramatic action that had been taken, Alex pointed to the back of the yacht and asked Trey to sit with her.

She suggested everyone continue fishing.

She gave Trey one of her ear buds and then called Johnnie.

After a brief "hello how are you," she thanked him for getting back up support for her. She then told him the body count in Chicago was on him and that he had now become the most dangerous miracle worker she knew.

Johnnie sputtered for a moment and then said that the execution was not his idea. Yes, he had talked to Adolfo to see if he could provide some protection. Adolfo had said he would take care of it.

Johnnie then said it had been Bill and Trevor who had suggested the idea of getting help from the "Angel on the hill."

He was just the messenger.

Alex continued to give him a hard time by telling him he had developed into a classic leader who always knew exactly how to deflect blame.

If he kept it up the cookie supply would dry up.

Then she got serious.

She thanked him for saving Trey and her life and that both of them owed him big time.

She asked how many cookies the big miracles would cost her.

Trey added that Johnnie should make a list of all the top restaurants he wanted to go to. He would make sure he got to all of them.

They both thanked him again.

Johnnie said by late in the afternoon on Sunday and for sure by dinner time, he would have a list of the "bad" and "the maybe bad" guys. He went on to say that all the known good guys were already on the list. The bad guys were being identified by their money and spending trail. The maybe bad guy's list might have a lot of good guys in it, but she would have to get some trusted Chicago police officer to ID them.

Alex let Johnnie know that she was going to spoil him as much as she could and that he should plan a vacation with Mary to a location of their choice. It would be her treat.

Alex looked at Trey and commented that they would now only need to deal with the bad cops but that was still a big and dangerous challenge.

Alex sat down at the table in the middle of the yacht's back deck. Matt poured her a large, iced tea and sat down with her. He asked if she was going to do any more fishing that day.

She responded that her big catch had occurred the day before and that she was going to sit and relax and think about how she and Trey should proceed in dealing with their assignment.

Alex relaxed, drank her iced tea, and enjoyed the gentle rocking of the boat and Nolan's excited voice as he caught a fish that took all his strength to reel in.

She had weathered the first storm of her assignment. Chicago was always facing storms blowing in from the lake.

She had grown up experiencing the Lake Michigan storms.

She knew that she and Trey would face many more storms in the Windy City as they went after the bad cops on its police force.

She hoped that Johnnie would continue to sprinkle his miracle powder and deliver the list he had promised.

20 Deep Dig

J ohnnie, Bill, and Trevor were not surprised when they got Alex's call to be on the lookout for hit men. They had done all they could to help but they were in Cincinnati and felt helpless.

They worried about Alex and reminisced about all the close calls she had survived.

They were holding their breaths on this case.

This one seemed more ominous than the rest had seemed.

They wondered if it was that on the other cases they had been more in the game than on the sideline. This was one they needed to be in the mainstream.

It was Saturday but they were sitting in a huddle room as Johnnie extracted data about the Chicago police members. He was able to directly access the information in the Chicago Police department personnel data base.

After putting each policeman into one of the three categories, Johnnie proceeded gathering information about each individual on the "Maybe Bad Guys" list. He soon had moved a significant number of names from that list to the "bad guys" list.

Johnnie sat in the huddle room and drank another cup of black coffee. He ate light so that he could continue his marathon research into the Chicago cops.

Bill and Travis were helping him by keeping files on their computers. They were operating together by sharing their computer accesses but staying off the internet. Johnnie was accessing every data base that he had access to and a few databases he had hacked.

He had already provided Alex the information about the top of the corrupt police food chain. He was now focused on identifying the bad cops. He assumed every cop was a bad one until he painted their financial picture. The ones that fell into the normal group were still put into a maybe bad category that he would scrutinize after identifying the obvious bad apples.

Bill was impressed with Johnnie's search skills. He was more impressed when Johnnie broke into the Mafia's data base and was able to get a list of all the cops that were taking money. The bad cops list grew dramatically, and the "maybe bad" cops list shrunk.

They were also able to see how much each bad cop was getting paid. Johnnie sorted the bad cops list and put it in the order of the ones getting the most to the ones getting the least.

They knew that Alex would be able to round up the bad guys in rapid order.

Bill organized the "Maybe" file on his computer. They were all using their computer capability to synchronize their work.

Trevor was capturing the "Bad" cop list.

This let Johnnie create temporary work files where he dumped information as he found it.

They were all surprised by the Chief's call. What the Chief was calling them about blew them away.

The Cartel's brutal protection of their "Cincinnati Black Annie Oakley" had resulted in the elimination of the entire Chicago Mafia leadership.

They were shocked.

They knew that they had been the ones that had put the execution into action.

Johnnie commented that he had not expected the kind of action that had taken place. It had eliminated the need for the extensive mafia information he had given to Alex on the previous Friday morning.

For the three of them, it underscored the importance of the work that they were doing.

The three of them decided to take a break and celebrate the elimination of a significant part of the threat to Alex and Trey.

Bill laughed and commented that the "White Angel on the Hill", the moniker that Alex had shared about the wife of the former Gulf Cartel leader, was also an avenging angel.

The request of help to her and the response was more than they had ever imagined.

Bill speculated that cartel must have used the moment to level the Chicago drug distribution playing field.

They all agreed that what they now should worry about was what the action of the leader of the "Bad Cops" group might take. That person was now on his own and might be driven to take drastic action.

Johnnie commented that he wanted to get the "Bad Cops" list into Alex's hands by Sunday evening.

He said that he was on a Marathon information hunt and would work around the clock.

He was pleased that Bill and Travis both arranged to stay with him and help. They said that there were two beds at the station available that they would nap in when they got too tired to work and they insisted that he at least take short naps throughout the night.

They had just finished their discussion when Alex called to thank them for having asked the "Angel on the Hill" for support.

Johnnie put the call on speaker mode.

They all smiled and chuckled as she said that the body count was theirs and not hers.

They commented that they had not asked for the kind of help that was delivered, and the body count should remain with the cartel.

Johnnie told Alex to expect the first draft of all the bad cops list by Sunday afternoon.

He praised the help he was getting from Bill and Travis.

Alex's thanked the three and the call ended.

Johnnie asked Bill and Trevor if they were still on for a marathon session.

When they said yes, he thanked them and went back to investigating each cop on the "Bad" guy's list. He had a step-by-step routine that was not as fast as he would have hoped but it spotted those cops that spent more than they were making on their official salaries.

The list of police member names that he had extracted from the mafia data base made the going much faster. He concentrated on the bank accounts and spending of those on the "Bad" guy's list.

The hours slowly crept by. Saturday night seemed to go on forever. He kept thanking Bill for coffee, donuts and the other snacks that were brought in.

Sunday morning Bill had him take a break and they went out to a local mom and pop diner for breakfast.

It was the break Johnnie needed, and it accelerated his progress.

Sunday sped by.

He saw the light at the end of the tunnel and knew he would be able to give Alex detailed lists of "Bad" and "Maybe Bad" cops as he had promised.

She would have enough information that could be presented to a prosecutor to charge and jail each bad guy. The money trail was obvious, and Johnnie was able to find where the money was kept for ninety percent of the bad guys. He planned on working on the remaining ten percent until he figured out where or how they were shielding their money.

Johnnie wisely concentrated of the money trail of the person at the top of the list.

He searched all the offshore banks that he could hack.

He hit the jackpot when he broke the security system of the Jamaican International Bank and found an account using Jesse Franklin's wife's maiden name.

21 Decision

Jesse knew he needed a Florida getaway. He had never felt as stressed out as he was at the moment.

After his wife agreed to a Florida get away, he turned his attention back to the two problems that remained in his lap.

It was clear that the Black detective assigned to root out corruption in the department had him nailed. He had to think through how he was going to handle that situation.

Gennaro had told him to relax and that he would take care of the detective and her partner. That assurance had reduced some of the stress but now he was aware that she had survived a surprise attack at her Cincinnati apartment and had killed two of Gennaro's top hit men. And within the last hour, she and her partner had killed two more of Gennaro's hit men in front of the police station.

She had turned his world on its head. He had never met a person that looked so pleasant and friendly but had proved to be so deadly.

Her personal confrontation in his office had to him been the derailment of a speeding train while it was crossing a bridge spanning the high cliffs and the engine crashing into the cliff face.

He was that engine.

The final straw that broke all his composure was the call of a multiple shooting at the Trucking office.

Alarm bells went off in his head.

He knew the address was that of, Gennaro Visentino, the mafia boss.

He rushed to the scene.

When he got there, it looked like a clean mass execution from the movie about the 1920's when Al "Scar Face" Capone and George "Bugs" Moan had battled it out..

The door to the meeting room had been kicked in and the bullet shell casings were laying where they had fallen when ejected. The execution weapons had been left on the floor. He was sure these weapons would not be easily traced and when they were the person who purchased them would likely be grandmothers or grandfathers that were unaware of how they would be used.

The coroner was still doing his preliminary crime scene evaluation.

Jessie stood watching and looked carefully around.

He noted that Gennaro was slumped back in his chair with multiple bullet holes that were still seeping blood.

A business card was in his hand.

A cold chill went down his back when he read, "From the Angel on the Hill." You should have heeded the warning."

He wondered who the Angel was.

He went into Gennaro's corner office at the end of the hallway. The view of the Lake Michigan caused him to stop. He wished he had an office with such a great view.

He was sure that Gennaro had chosen that specific office for the view. He had listened to many of his reminiscences of his parent's home and the view and the smells of the sea.

He saw a paper lying face down on the desk and turned it over.

As he read it another chill went down his back.

It warned Gennaro to not interfere or hamper the work of Alex Evercrest. He was to stand back or face serious consequences.

Jesse stood looking out on the lake.

He put what he had just witnessed in the meeting room as a serious consequence.

He realized that he now had no mafia protection.

He felt naked, exposed and on the verge of losing everything.

He returned to the office and put one of his research resources on the hunt for where the detective was staying and how she would get to the station.

He would show that detective that he had a powerful information network too.

He planned on finishing what Gennaro had promised to do. He felt that he was not in as much danger from the Cartel as Genraro had been.

He needed to eliminate this upstart detective at all cost.

His research resource informed him that the detective had attended Northwestern University and had driven a black Jag to school. The Jag was still registered to her name in the State of Illinois. The address on the registration was that of her parents in Evanston.

Jesse studied the various routes she could chose to come to the station. He decided that the fastest route would be to stay on Shore Drive all the way to the station.

He studied the map and located a turn in the road where a parked car would be visible only at the last moment. He was certain that he had found a way to solve his problem.

The simple set up of having a disabled car with the hood up would catch her by surprise and he selected a location where she would not have time to react.

He still had a couple of good mafia connections, and he conclude he would get their support by positioning his idea to rid himself of this Cincinnati detective by letting them know that she had gotten their bosses killed.

He had an eager participant to an assassination when the hit man found out that his compatriots had been killed because of her.

Gennaro had failed but he planned to finish the job. He was not going to give the "Black Cincinnati bi_ _ _ " a chance to nail him.

He figured that if it worked, he could continue running his internal group of cops as usual.

However, he also planned to process his retirement papers and be ready to leave the state.

It was late for a Friday and time to go home. By noon on Monday his choice would be clear.

Once he got home, he sat sipping on his beer as he watched his wife prepare the evening meal.

He was faced with the fact that he was caught, and his mafia protector was dead, and he had to act to save himself.

The cash from the mafia connection was icing on his cake. The cake was the protection money his network of crooked cops got from all the business owners. He would be able to save the bigger part of his cash flow.

If the ambush was successful, he could continue doing business as usual.

However, he was going to take the precaution of submitting his resignation and fast tracking its approval on Monday morning.

If the ambush failed, he would need to make his departure and get out of Dodge. He figured life in his Florida condo would be enjoyable.

He had several hundred million dollars accessible in his offshore account.

He arrived to work early on Monday. It took him only a short time to fill out his retirement papers.

He personally walked them through, and when they were complete and he had them in his hand, he went to the cafeteria for breakfast.

He figured he would chat with his buddies and await the kill confirmation call that he expected from the setup that he had arranged.

She would be dead, and he would remain in control of his kingdom.

He did not get the expected call. He figured that the shooting might not have worked out as planned but he hoped that she was at least critically wounded.

He returned to his office to make sure his departure was assured.

Little did Jesse know that his departure would indeed happen on this day, but it was not the departure he had anticipated.

22 *Foiled*

*A*fter a great day out on the Lake, followed by a relaxing time around the pool and a great fish dinner prepared by her mother and Lindsey, Alex excused herself and went up to bed early.

She had shared her concerns with Matt about what actions the bad cops might take in the coming weeks.

Her intuition was nagging her. She mentioned that to him.

He told her to listen to her intuition.

She woke up several times during the night with lingering snippets of shooting scenes.

It was clear to her that she was experiencing a random collage of past shootings.

In every scene she was too slow to act, and she saved herself by waking up.

She recognized the night as a series of nightmares. Each seemed to be a warning of some unanticipated action.

In the morning, she went down to breakfast and was waiting on a fried shredded cabbage, infused with egg, breakfast that her mother insisted she fix for her.

She was more interested in the coffee and getting to a fully alert state.

Her intuition had the hair on the back of her neck feeling like it was standing up like that of a mad Doberman attack hound.

When Trey came into the kitchen her mother offered to fix him the same thing that she was fixing for Alex.

He accepted and sat down with his cup of coffee.

She put Alex's breakfast on the table and proceeded to cook Trey's breakfast.

Trey seemed very calm and rested to Alex. She asked him how he had slept, and he replied, "like a baby."

When he asked her about her night, she replied that she slept like a colicky baby.

He simply said, "Oh! Sorry to hear that."

When she saw that Trey was done with his breakfast. She got up and led the way into the garage. Her black Jag sparkled as she turned on the lights.

Her father had let her know that he had it serviced, and it was ready to go.

The weather was mild, and she decided to drive with the top down.

She asked Trey if he was OK with that.

He smiled and turned his cap backwards and said that he would suffer through it.

She took the same road she had driven many times to school. She planned to drive past the university and continued down along lake shore drive to the station.

Suddenly the hair on the back of her neck stood up.

She let Trey know about it and that he should be ready to take the wheel if she asked. She took her new weapon issued to her by the state of Illinois and put it on her lap. She had not yet had a chance to fire it.

She hoped that it fired accurately.

Just past the campus where the road turned and went under an overpass, she spotted a car with its hood up.

She asked Trey to take the wheel. She took her foot off the gas as she approached the car. As she came even with the car, she spotted the gunman raising his weapon to shoot. She stepped on the brakes as she shot him three times.

The shooter's gun went off, but it was still pointed downward, and the bullet hit the road.

Alex stopped the car and backed it up behind the car with the raised hood.

She approached the car as if there might be a second person inside.

It was empty.

She checked the shooter.

He was dead.

She had not dared to spare him.

Alex asked Trey to wait for fifteen minutes and then call the police dispatcher to let them know about the shooting.

She asked Trye if he was willing to stay on the scene while she went immediately go to get the Assistant Chief before he could escape.

She felt certain that he had set up the attempt to kill them.

She arrived at the station and went straight to where the Grizzley old Sargent was sitting at his desk. She asked if he were willing to be her back up as she made an arrest of the Department Deputy Chief.

After making sure she wasn't joking.

He gave a gruff chuckle and said he would love to back her up as she nailed the son of a B....

She asked him to first take her to the Police Chief. She went past the receptionist that wanted her to come back later. She walked in and gave the Chief of Police the arrest order for the Deputy Police Chief.

He looked at the order and said, "you have got to be kidding."

Alex presented the list of bad cops.

Again, she again got, "you have got to be kidding," exclamation.

He looked at her and commented that she was working at the speed of light and asked how she had gotten all the information so quickly.

She replied that she had a super sleuth analysist that delivered miracles at the speed of light.

The information was all there for the person doing the right search.

She then said she was going to meet with his Deputy Police Chief and would arrest him and asked for two trustworthy officers to take him to a holding cell.

She then said she was on her way to the Deputy Chief's office to make the arrest.

The grizzly sergeant led the way. Alex followed.

The Chief asked his support to send two policemen to the Assistant Chief's office and then hurried to catch up to where Alex had stopped and was waiting for him.

Jesse was surprised when the door to his office opened. He was about to give the old cop walking in a piece of his mind when he spotted his nemesis behind him.

He did not see the third person.

He stood up and waved his retirement papers.

He commented that he had just gotten them approved and his boss had sign off on them.

Jesse had a smug look on his face.

He gave her a smile and again waved his retirement papers and let her know that he had retired and was just getting ready to leave the station.

He let her know she could find him in Florida if she wanted to ask him any questions.

Alex thanked him for taking the action that made his arrest even easier. She read him his Miranda rights and had the sergeant hand cuff him.

The two requested policeman arrived, and the Chief told them to take the Assistant Chief to a holding cell. They were to stand by and make sure that nothing happened to the Assistant Chief.

As Jesse was about to be led out, Alex let him know that he would be standing in front of a judge that morning and would most likely spend a few days in a holding cell right at the station before being transferred to a state facility to await his trial.

She let him know that she had the location of his offshore account and that she would be able to transfer it all into a holding account that she had created. She wanted him to know that he would never get to spend the money that he had illegally gained by strong arming the small business owners in Chicago.

That money was no more.

Once he had been taken away, she called Johnnie and asked him to set up an account for her and to transfer the money that was in Jamaica to an account in Chicago. Once that was done, he was to send the information to the Lieutenant Governor's support.

Alex asked the old sergeant if the two cops escorting the Assistant Chief were good cops and got an affirmative nod.

She then asked his name and asked him if he would like to work with her in rooting out the bad cops.

She smiled when he asked her why she thought he was a good cop.

She replied that she figured a cop that was as mean as he seemed to be had to be a good cop.

That got a laugh from him. He introduced himself as Mike Strimble.

Alex said that she was pleased to be able to work with him. They shook hands before leaving Assistant Chief's office.

23 Resolution

*A*lex walked to the office that she and Trey had been assigned.

She asked Mike to identify two additional officers to work with them.

She then sent a list of officers for whom she wanted arrest warrants to the Lieutenants Governor's office.

Trey walked in and after making introductions Alex asked Mike where about two hundred individuals could be placed as they awaited trial.

Mike gave a whistle when he heard the number and said that they would have to be sent to Statesville Correctional Center. Even then he would have to check to see if they currently had enough capacity available.

Alex asked Mike to find out what the statewide capacity availability happened to be. She said that the current number of two hundred was the tip of the iceberg.

Alex then asked Mike to set up transport that could move twenty people a day to a jail facility.

She let him know that she was going to take out the top offenders immediately but that she expected many more as well.

Finally, she asked him to identify the number of good cops needed to make it all happen.

She then went on and let him know that once he had that list, he was to take it to the Chief of Police and let him know that she was requesting the help he had promised.

She let Mike know that he was not to accept a no to the list he presented. She let Mike know that she held a rank higher than his Chief.

She looked at the clock on the wall and told Trey that they had a lunch meeting with their boss.

They went to the designated restaurant and were escorted to a private meeting room.

Jane was by herself, but she was on the phone shaking her head.

She got off the phone and stood up and gave Alex a hug.

She shook hands with Trey and then pointed to a table that was set for three.

Once they were seated, she asked what Alex would like to drink and said that she had arranged for them to have a choice of red meat, fish, or chicken.

Alex said that she would like to order a lamb chop and iced tea.

Trey selected an order of brisket, mashed potatoes with gravy.

He also chose iced tea.

Once the orders were in, Jane said that she wanted to verify what her support had called her about.

She asked if Alex had requested arrest warrants for two hundred and three police officers.

Alex nodded and said that she would like to have them as soon as possible and she wanted space reserved for them at Statesville Correctional Center.

She would also need enough judges lined up to process the arrests and set trial dates.

Jane said that she would have her office take the requested action.

She then asked about the bank account that her support had set up that made her office the holder of the account and the two hundred million or so dollars that had been mysteriously transferred in from a bank in Jamaica.

Alex said that was money that the Assistant Chief of Police had robbed from the businesses in Chicago and she had it transferred to Jane so that she and the State of Illinois could decide how it should be spent in helping the small businesses in Chicago.

Jane shook her head.

She let Alex know that she had not dreamt of getting that much money back and would need to think how it should be utilized.

She made the comment that she had felt that Alex had gotten the upper hand in their negotiations, and she remembered Alex's comments about the good deal she was getting.

She said that she would like to go on record that she now saw it not as a great deal but the best that she had ever negotiated.

She then asked what there was left to do.

Lunch arrived and Alex suggested they enjoy lunch and get into the details after it was over.

After lunch, Alex ordered a cup of green tea.

She then pointed out that she and Trey would be going to court to support the prosecutors that would be charging the bad cops.

She would have her analyst preparing the materials that the prosecutors would need to get convictions.

When Jane asked her how long it would take to process two hundred bad cops, Alex replied that the time would depend on how many judges and prosecutors the state of Illinois assigned to handle the situation.

Alex told Jane that she was taking the top bad cops off the streets and out of the offices. But her analyst had let her know that he had more than three thousand personnel on the "Bad Cops" and "Maybe Bad Cops" list.

Processing them all would take several months.

Getting them into holding cells and then charged would again depend on Jane's ability to line up judges and prosecutors.

Alex told her that she and Trey would be doing much of the continuing activity from her home office.

She added that she had hired a driver and an armored limo to drive to and from meetings and to court appearances.

She would also arrange to have the good cops providing her protection in the coming few months.

She asked Jane if she was satisfied with her new employees and that she would have them on hand until all the bad guys were all charged and put behind bars.

Jane said that she had known her mother since the college years, and she had always been impressed with her, but she would have to let her good friend know that her daughter had bested her in how to break the blue barrier and if her guess was right in having connections that had eliminated the current Mafia leadership.

She told Alex that she had let her support know to do anything that was needing doing and that she had told her entire organization to help as requested.

Alex thanked her for the support.

She let Jane know that she was invited her to go fishing on the upcoming weekend.

The End

Preview of: Country Road

Country Road

1 SLATE

*E*than was looking forward to a late afternoon indulgence that he had come to enjoy every month. It always raised his adrenalin level and the world around him slowed to a pace where his actions seemed amplified.

The begging and pleading made it feel even better.

Then at the end he often tortured the victim before finally killing her.

This was a way of life that had evolved in a natural organic way. He was not sure how it had come to him and how he had perfected the technique that allowed him to satisfy his desire without getting caught but he had.

He had now experienced multiple years of such monthly enjoyment.

He waited until there were no cars in sight and then drove his four by four off the highway into the dense forest.

201

He went in as far as he could before stopping.

He got out and made sure that the truck was not visible.

His three SLATE members piled out carrying their partially consumed beers.

He preferred not to drink before having sex.

He took the tarp off the bed of the truck where the husband and woman were tied.

He stood quietly for a moment enjoying the sight

He had selected a good looking, young well bosomed Mexican woman.

A few weeks ago, he had spotted her shopping at the supermarket and had followed her home.

He had learned that she and her husband were staying with her sister until they could appear in court and ask for official entrance into the US.

The more he learned about her the better prospect she became. He would have preferred to have nabbed her without her husband, but he had accompanied her to the market that morning and now he would be part of the fun.

He figured it would fun to make the husband watch as his wife was repeatedly raped.

He was especially looking forward to the moment that he cut out her tongue and stuffed it into the husband's mouth.

The more he thought about it the more ways he thought of making her husband suffer.

He was sure that other guys would come up with even weirder scenarios.

He signaled his buddies to get the two out of the pickup.

He looked over to where the slender, well bosomed young Mexican woman was on her knees cowering. Her husband had his hands zip locked in front of him and was trying to console her. He wondered what the husband could possibly be telling her.

He laughed to himself and quietly said, "everything is going to be alright."

He and his fellow SLATE members were celebrating their second year as a part of a national network set up by his buddy, Isaac in Ohio.

It had been a good two years and their motto of "no body, no crime" had proved to be true.

They had so far operated undetected.

He knew it was a matter of selecting the victim carefully.

They would all have their way with this bitch, and then they would eliminate both her and her husband.

His followers were always ready for the next monthly engagement. They each took turns selecting the next conquest and they always chose a very out of the way location to hold their celebration event.

They never returned to any of the previous locations.

The missing women never made the news or if they did the attention almost immediately faded.

All the chapters of SLATE reported the same phenomena.

Ethan had organized SLATE with his six college buddies, but he learned college was not for him.

A windblown rainstorm spitting hail the size of marbles had leveled trees for miles and had presented him an opportunity to be on a tree clearance crew and to make what he felt at the time was a small fortune.

He never went back to college.

He concentrated on using what seemed like a good income in funding the SLATE activities.

His buddies from the south left school at about the same time.

His best friend that now lived in Ohio and his far away friend from Oregon both stayed and graduated.

When he later learned that his income was close to or more than they made he felt justified in having dropped out.

The year after his best buddy graduated, Ethan got them together and they each set up SLATE their hometowns. They all embraced the goal of having sex with women of their choosing whenever they chose and in the way they chose to have it.

They developed several scenarios of how they would have any woman they chose.

The common elements that spanned all scenarios was that the woman had to be young, good looking but low in the social ladder and that each scenario culminated with no witnesses.

Simply put they believed in the saying, "no body, no witness, no crime."

It worked better than anyone of them expected.

Preview of: Country Road

It was the beginning of SLATE's active period, and it spread across the country from Ohio to Washington State.

This afternoon his members complimented him on the fact that he had selected a beauty. They were eager to get to the forest and begin the orgy.

They got excited when he described how he planned the end of the session.

One of the members said that he wanted to tongue kiss her before he cut out her tongue.

They had jumped out and were ready to begin but he held them back as he told them to take their time and enjoy the celebration.

He clarified who was to do the next selection for the coming month's woman.

He then asked where they should hold the next event.

He also wanted the two graves for this event to be dug before the partying began so that at the end they could quickly clean up and leave the area.

He said he wanted to leave the place looking as if no one had been there.

He stood by as the graves were dug down about five feet. There were no rocks in the area to put immediately on top of the dead bodies but he had brought out six bags of concrete that he would dump on top of them.

That would form a solid layer and would keep the odor of the decaying bodies from being noticeable.

As he turned toward the young woman she jumped up and began to run.

He was surprised at her speed.

He pulled up her husband, shoved him, and told him to stop his wife or he would shoot him on the spot.

He pointed to where she was running and told his three members to catch her, but they should not shoot either of the two.

He ran after the five running figures but held back in case she turned in some new direction.

He could hear her husband shouting at her, but he could not hear what he was saying and even if would have, he didn't know any Spanish.

He noted that she was slowly losing ground to his three members.

They would have her in less than a few minutes.

Then he spotted a black sports car driving slowly along the narrow road that he knew led to an apple orchard.

It seemed that the young woman had also seen the car because she sped up and ran towards it.

He stopped at the edge of the forest and watched as a young rather attractive Black woman who was driving almost hit the running woman.

He watched as she jumped out of the convertible and shouted that she was a sheriff and told everyone to stop and get down on their knees.

His members were ready for a fight and as they raised their weapons, the Black woman blew the gun out of one member's hand, shot the second in the chest and was ready to shoot the third when he dropped his gun and got down on his knees.

Ethan saw the husband trying to say something but the woman claiming to be a sheriff waved her gun to indicate he get down on his knees as well.

Ethan faded back into the forest. He watched as a young, tall Black man hand cuffed the third member and then turned his attention to the second member who had blood slowly turning his t-shirt red. He could hear the member who was holding his right hand with his left hand repeating over and over again, "you bitch, you blew off my finger."

It was clear to Ethan that the Black woman was in charge and in command.

He decided that it was time to get back to the truck and leave while the leaving was good. He picked up everything that he had brought in and threw it in the back of the pickup and put the bed cover back on.

He drove slowly back through the forest to the highway. He waited until there were no cars and then drove onto the highway.

Less than mile later he watched as a highway patrol followed by an ambulance sped by with lights flashing and sirens blaring.

He knew that he had left just in time.

He hoped that the SLATE members remembered that they had pledged silence about what went on in SLATE. But he decided that he would get his escape trunk, put it in the back of the pickup and leave for a random destination that he would select when he was ready to abandon his apartment.

He wondered who the Black bitch happened to be and vowed to take care of her at some future time.

Little did he know who would take care of whom.

2 Apple Picking

Alex was enjoying what she considered to be one of the few vacation trips to her parents' home. Matt had come along which made it special. The entire family had gone out fishing to their favorite location on the lake and had caught several large bass.

Her mother, a globally recognized chef, prepared several of the catch for their evening dinner.

They had enjoyed an evening by the pool and had caught up with what was happening.

They all commented on the fact that the events of the previous cases had been too close to home and of such danger that they hoped that future cases would be located in some other location.

Alex's mother promised that she would never get Alex involved in another case like the one in Chicago.

This day had started with she and Matt having a late breakfast at the Harbor Restaurant.

They had then taken a walk along the beach.

Now the two of them were going to pick apples at a farm where Alex had gone several times with her parents when she was young.

She was driving much slower than normal and enjoying the breeze blowing through her hair.

The road from the highway back to the "Northern Illinois Apple Haven" wound through a dense forest on a narrow road.

Alex had fond memories riding through the forest to go and pick apples with her parents.

She was now looking forward to sharing that experience with Matt.

She wanted to create memories that the two of them could look forward to.

Matt had commented that every time he went out on the lake fishing, he remembered the time when they were almost gunned down by the helicopter gun ship, her setting the coal barge on fire when she killed the helicopter pilot and he crashed into the coal.

He said that was a memory that they shared and that neither of them was likely to forget.

Alex replied that she wanted to create more pleasurable memories then having gunships trying to kill them and setting a coal barge on fire.

The road had been paved since the last time she had been on it, but it was still a one lane narrow road.

The forest that it ran through had grown thicker. Tall dark green pine and at this time of year, punctuated by brown leafy, large oaks and yellow and red leafed maples, was an awe-inspiring sight just as she remembered it to be.

She was slowly driving her beloved, black twelve-cylinder, convertible Jaguar along the lane toward the apple farm.

She had just given Matt's hand a squeeze and was about to share her feelings when, a woman screaming for help in Spanish, ran in front of her car.

She stomped on the brakes and was able to stop just short of hitting her.

She took in the four men chasing the young woman, as she took her weapon and Illinois State Police badge from her purse.

She asked Matt to take the gun in the glove compartment and back her up.

She made the comment that he was as good a shot as she was and that he should be ready to shoot at her command.

Matt did not say a word, but he knew that she was over stating his capability and underplaying hers.

He had watched her shoot blindfolded when her instructor challenged to her do so. She had positioned herself as the blind fold was put on and had then rapidly fired her revolver seven times. The bullets made a ring around the center of the target, and she had put the seventh-round dead center.

It was something that was impossible to forget.

He knew that she never missed that for which she aimed.

He was not only slower than she, but he also could not match her ability to place her shots.

He took the weapon and knelt and aimed over the top of the car hood.

He listened as Alex told everyone to stop as she declared her status as an Illinois sheriff. She then told everyone to drop their weapons and get on their knees.

Matt noted that the first person had his hands ziplocked in front of him but did as he was told.

Alex repeated her command and as all three of the other chasers raised their guns, she shot the gun out of the first person's hand, she shot the second person in the left chest and was about to take the next shot, but the third person dropped his gun and got on his knees.

Matt watched as Alex collected the weapons and brought them to the side of the car.

She then walked over to the person she had shot second and took in the blood oozing out.

She called for him to bring the first aid kit and see what he could do for the person on the ground.

The first person she shot was down on his knees moaning and holding his right hand with his left hand.

He listened as he cursed her for shooting off the index finger of his right hand.

She nodded and told him to lay on his back and put his right hand in the air and the pain would decrease.

She walked over to where the young woman being chased had knelt down with the first person that had been chasing her.

She listened briefly to the young woman.

Matt realized that the young woman was saying everything in Spanish.

Then somewhat surprised, he heard Alex reply in Spanish that the two of them were safe and that she needed to make several calls to get help.

She dialed 911 and explained the situation and made sure that the operator on the line knew where they were located and that an ambulance was needed as well as transport for three prisoners and two victims.

She then went to the car and took a pair of handcuffs from her purse.

She had the third would be shooter move over to the first shooter and had him lay down beside the first shooter. She handcuffed them together.

Matt had stopped the bleeding of the second shooter who had passed out.

Alex returned to the two that had been chased and asked for an explanation.

She listened as the young woman explained that the two of them had been kidnapped and brought to the forest. She was to have been "used" by her abductor and the three that had chased them.

Alex asked about the fourth person.

She said that she had only seen the three that were on the ground.

Alex stood up and looked at the forest and decided she needed to make certain that the fourth person was no longer around.

She asked Matt whether he could handle the situation at the road.

She felt better about the situation as her ears captured the wailing of the sirens.

She set out on a slow jog into the woods.

Her senses were at full alert.

Her path took her straight in. She came to where two pits had been dug. It was clear to her that they were to be graves.

She began jogging a circular pattern looking for a sign of tire tracks. On the second loop she came across the tracks of a truck that had duel wheels on the back. She hoped that the double wheels would provide a way to narrow the number of trucks she might end up looking for.

She stopped and began to slowly walk back toward her car. She was on the phone with her Illinois boss, the Lieutenant Governor, when a sheriff with his gun drawn came toward her. She held up her badge and let him know that she was a Marshal in the Lieutenant Governor's staff and that her boss was on the line.

He took the phone and listened as he was informed that he was to listen carefully to and follow the instructions of Special Marshall Alex Evercrest.

He handed back her phone and smiled.

He let her know that he had followed the case where she had cleaned up the Chicago Police Department and thanked her for doing it.

Alex asked him to make the whole area a crime scene. She pointed back toward where the truck tire tracks were located and said that she had planted a stick to mark the spot. She took him by what she said she thought were to have been the graves of the young woman and her husband.

The two of them returned to where her car was parked.

Alex saw that the ambulance personnel were talking with Matt.

He walked over to her and said that both the police and the ambulance personnel needed to get the handcuffs removed.

Alex went to her purse and gave Matt the keys.

She asked the sheriff if he would take responsibility for the young woman and her husband.

She suggested that both of them needed to go to the hospital, and they needed to stay in protective custody because the fourth person that had escaped might want to silence them.

She asked that once everything settled down, he should call her and let her know where she could interview the two victims.

She let him know that she was going to go pick a bushel of apples and then go back to the house she was raised in.

The officer got her address and phone number and told her he would keep her informed.

Thank you for reading this far.

To read more of: Country Road Go to:

https://Remwriter95.net/

About the Author

Ronald E. Mueller
remwriter95@gmail.com

Ron grew up in what is now Flint River State Park in Southeast Iowa. The 170-year-old house Ron lived in is built into a hillside. It faces a 125-foot-high cliff towering over the little Flint River. The house and the land talked to him about; the passing of time, the struggle to conquer the land, the struggles people faced and the wonder of nature.

He climbed the cliffs, crawled into the caves, dove from the swimming rock, collected clams from the bottom of the pond, gigged and skinned frogs for their legs. He trapped muskrats for fur, hunted raccoon in the dead of night, and with only a stick hunted rabbits in the dead of winter.

His young life was outdoors, and nature tested him.

He walked to a one room stone schoolhouse uphill both ways. A stern but warm-hearted teacher, Mrs. Henry was instrumental in shaping his character as she shepherded him from the fourth to the eighth grade.

It was a great way to grow up.

Ron graduated from Burlington, High School, went to Vietnam in the Navy. He graduated from The University of South Florida with an master's degree in engineering, worked for thirty eight years for Procter and Gamble, traveled around the world thirty times.

He has remained happily married for more than fifty years. His daughter and his two sons are all successful and his three grandchildren have all graduated.

His wife has humored and supported him as he became a full time professional story teller.

He has come to realize that he is, what is known as, a Cozy writer. Excitement and adventure but little guts and gore. His heroine or hero suffer a little but live happily ever after.

His experiences inter-twined with snippets of fantasy lend themselves to the adventures he leads the reader through.

Books by the Author

Books by Ron Mueller

The Taelo Series
Taelo: The Early Years
Taelo: The Golden Feather
Taelo: Journey of Discovery
Taelo: Dangerous Passage
Taelo: Condor Clan Slingers
Taelo: Circumvention
Taelo: The Journey of Sages
Taelo: Collection
Taelo: Future Leaders Journey

A Taelo Story:
White Swan and Quiet Pheasant
The Child's Name
Floating Cloud
Quiet Rabbit
Busy Bee
Little Otter & Talking Wren
Broken Spear
Burley Bear & Meadow Flower
Taelo Story Collection

Science Fiction
The Savitar Series:
Journey's End
Savitar
Confluence
Savitar Series Collection

Bram Nielson Series
The Fold
The Message
Fold Wormhole
Negative Fold
Ripples in Time
Bram Nielson Collection

Single Science Fiction Books:
Current Past and Future
The Event
The Door
Viajante 7

https://www.Remwriter95.net/

Published by: Around the World Publishing LLC.